The Tomb of Gods: Book One

The Gorgon

and

The Witch

H.T. Mejia

H.T. Mejia

Other works by H.T. Mejia

The Requiem of Kora duology:

Book One: The Ballad of Wrath and Death

Book Two: A Psalm of Reaping

To whom it may concern,
There is always a choice. Sometimes they are easy to make,
sometimes they are difficult, and sometimes we regret them. But
always, there is a choice.

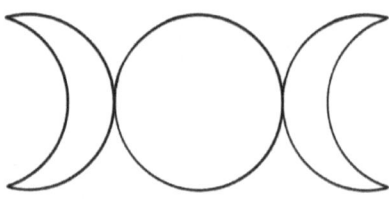

Trigger Warnings

This book contains material some readers may find triggering, including conversations about sexual assault and abuse. You will find physical violence, explicit language, and sexually explicit scenes within these pages.

The Gorgon

and

The Witch

H.T. Mejia

Prologue

Curious, how time whittles away at the things around us– changing them right before our eyes.

I glanced around the room. There was once a large, canopy bed there, wardrobes and looking glasses. In their place was a new bed, much smaller and lower to the ground than the other had been, and a chest full of toys. On the far side of the room sat an ornately carved rocking chair.

Persephone swayed in the chair, her voice filling the room as she sang a haunting lullaby. Red hair cascaded over her shoulders, the tight curls nearly touching the floor. Zagreus, still a small boy, was wrapped tightly in her arms, his hands resting atop her stomach, which housed another babe.

My lips twitched up into a smile. In a blink I had watched her grow from a small, ornery child with fiery hair to a Goddess who was both selfless and terrifying. The Goddess of Spring, the Herald of Life and the Bringer of Death. Queen of the Underworld. Yet, some time ago she had gone by a different name.

Kora.

I raked my fingers through my unbound waves and leaned against the ivy covered wall of the nursery. I remembered a time when the Underworld could not sustain life the way it did with Persephone ruling over it. A time when all it had to offer was iron and desolation.

The Underworld and the queen who ruled over it was not all that had changed, though. Its king, the other Gods, and the Shades of those who died were also different. Olympus changed, along with the Gods who call it their home.

And me.

My eyes met Persephone's and happiness bloomed across her face.

I had become a different God somewhere along the way, though I'm not sure I could say when I changed. But it was undeniable.

I had many names. Witch, Goddess, Titan. Mother, Maiden, Crone. The Torch Bearer, She Who Wanders at Night, The Moon Mistress. Hecate; the Goddess of Magic and Darkness–

And most recently: Aunt.

Aunt Hecate, the boy called me.

Zagreus was young, but still, he was a wild boy. The earth and the animals who dwelled there called to his very soul, just as they did for his mother. He longed to be above, running bare foot through the grass. As untamed as he was, his mind was free of the Wrath that twisted Persephone in a way that made mortals tremble.

10

We could not be sure about the babe still growing in her womb.

Persephone's Wrath was uncharted territory– something new to all of us who came before her. We had no idea how it would manifest, if it even did, in the children. That sliver of the unknown had scared me when Zagreus was still in her womb, but as soon as she had placed the boy in my arms, my heart swelled and I no longer feared what the future would hold for him.

I loved him, and I knew I would love the next babe as well.

How strange life had turned out; how twisted and winding it had been– like a river. I had stood at many crossroads, and been left walking in random directions with only my faith in The Fates to guide me.

My heart had been filled with love over and over, just as it had been broken time and time again. I could only imagine what other surprises the future would hold for all of us, but sitting there, looking at Persephone and Zagreus…

I did not fear it.

I welcomed whatever was to be with open arms, beckoning it to come to me.

"Hecate," Persephone said softly. My eyes snapped up to hers and she smiled. "What are you thinking?"

"Nothing," I said.

In truth, I was thinking of everything. Every pivotal moment I had ever had; every time I stood on the edge of a drastic change in my life, teetering either way before falling face first into something that would forever decide the course of my future.

I was thinking about *everything*.

1.

The Hermit

A loud wailing violently ripped me from my dreamless sleep. The cries rang through the air, a broken, grieving sound.

It was the Gorgon again.

She wandered the vast wastes of the Underworld, interrupting my sleep and distracting me from my craft, weeping and howling at the gray sky.

I groaned, rubbing my eyes.

How the Gorgon managed to evade The Furies' rabid attacks was an act of The Fates. She must have quickly learned where the lines of their territory ended. I hadn't a clue how she had yet to anger Hades with her cries, though. His bleeding heart for the neglected and discarded would carry her only so far before he tired of it.

I was already tired of it.

Hades had to consider the balance of his land when deciding to enact his fury and his retribution. If he allowed himself to take the lives of everyone who angered him, the Underworld would be overflowing with shades, and there was limited space in Taratarus for prisoners.

But the ebb and flow of the Underworld was no concern of mine.

I had taken the lives of many mortals, dooming their souls to wander as a shade forever. But each life I had taken deserved my vengeance. Unlike some of the other Gods, who flaunted their powers and let their anger devour needlessly, I chose carefully when cutting mortals down.

My favored punishment of the vile was not taking their lives, but shifting their bodies into small and insignificant beings who would know no death. They would be forced to live their days with their minds trapped in the body of an animal, lost to their thoughts with no way to speak or communicate.

I did not only use that magic to punish. Sometimes it was a gift. A reprieve from the harsh world that threatened to consume someone.

I sat up, pushing the covers off of my body and my eyes drifted to the black, shaggy dog laying next to me. Her gaze, far more aware than normal dogs, lifted to mine.

Hecuba was the perfect example of how my dark magic could be the start of a beautiful life, rather than the end of it.

She let out a soft whine, her bushy tail thumping against the bed. Her wordless pleas were clear on her face. *"Have mercy,"* she would have said if she could speak. *"A wounded heart cannot heal on its own."*

"It is not my place to coddle those who incurred the wrath of the other Gods, Hecuba."

I forced my tired body out of the bed, my legs still weak and my mind foggy. The rest of my dogs laid in a tangled heap on the floor beside me. I stepped around them, careful of their gangly legs and long tails. They were naturally born dogs, unlike Hecuba, but I loved them all the same.

Another wail broke the silence as I snatched a black robe from a rusty hook on the wall and wrapped it around my body. I would end her sorrowful cries one way or another.

Bottles of liquids and herbs clanked against each other as I rummaged for anything I could use to shield my eyes from the stare of the Gorgon that promised death. Not death *for me*, per se, but closer to it than I wished to get.

I pulled a strip of purple cloth from under a dusty book and shook it off. It wasn't perfect by any means, but it would have to do.

The cries continued, much louder than they had been before, as I shoved my boots on and swung my door open. My eyes widened as they fell on the back of the Gorgon.

Her clothes were tattered and torn, the snakes atop her head pulling aggressively, as if they too wished to free themselves of her. My gaze drifted down her body, catching on every inch of exposed green skin.

She must have been attacked, judging by the look of her dress. Perhaps The Furies had gotten ahold of her, after all. Not that I could blame them, her constant sobbing had brought me to that very point myself.

But as I stood there, looking at her, all of the anger I had moments before melted away.

14

I clenched the strip of cloth in my fist.

No.

She had been the source of my anguish for weeks, causing me to seek refuge in the mortal lands. I did not wish to spend anymore of my time in the world above. Humans were sometimes more vile and putrid than the Gods.

I shook my head, shooing away the last of my sympathy for the Gorgon, and wrapped the cloth around my eyes. My boot thumped against the black iron ground as I stepped off of my porch, heading toward the sound of the battered beast ahead.

Her crying quieted until she was sniffling. "Is someone there?"

She sounded kind and soft, despite whatever she had done to anger Athena to the point of such a cruel punishment. My eyes squeezed shut beneath their cover, my fists balling at my sides.

"Yes." I took another step toward her.

"Please, stop!" Her tone was shrill, making me freeze. "Please don't look at me. Go away!"

Her voice was muffled. Was her face buried in her hands?

"I have no intention of looking at you, Gorgon. I only came to tell you that you must take your sorrow elsewhere. If I have to listen to another minute of it, I will remove your head."

"I'm sorry," she said after a long pause. "I did not mean to disturb you."

"Well, you did!" I snapped.

She shifted against the iron ground, and I strained my ears to make sure I could hear her leave, but I could not.

"It's terribly lonely down here," she said quietly.

My lips pulled down into a frown. "It was before you got here."

Her footsteps were soft against the iron, but she was stepping *toward* me. "Is there somewhere I might stay?"

A heavy sigh left my mouth before I could stop it. "I do not know. That is not my business. However, you cannot stay here– I have heard quite enough out of you."

I expected her to take the hint and leave, but she spoke again. "I've been sleeping on the hard ground. Surely you must know somewhere I can live here?"

A muscle in my jaw ticked. "Listen, Gorgon–"

"Medusa," she corrected. "My name is Medusa."

"I do not care to know your name, *Gorgon*. Leave, before you anger me further."

"I just–"

"Have you not angered enough Gods for one lifetime?"

I did not have to see her to know she recoiled from my words– I could feel it. Guilt tried to work its way into my heart, but I shoved it down. I had decided long ago I would not let guilt rule my life.

Her soft steps began receding, and I reached up to lift the cloth from my eyes. I watched her walk away from me, her arms wrapped tightly around herself. The snakes atop her head had settled slightly, and I could have sworn they were watching me back as she left.

"Gorgons," I muttered under my breath.

I turned on my heel and stomped back into my small cabin, slamming the worn door behind me. My gaze dropped to the pack of dogs that stood waiting for me to return to bed. Hecuba had sadness in her large brown eyes.

"Don't look at me like that." I reached out and patted the top of her head.

I did not desire company or friends, save the animals I took in. Most of my life had been spent alone, and that was exactly how I preferred it.

The Gorgon had done something to anger Athena, and that was not my fault. She could figure her own way around the Underworld, as all of the creatures cast there before her had.

I tossed my robe onto the floor, kicking the boots off of my feet, and then crawled back into the bed. Hecuba jumped up and flopped herself across my body. I closed my eyes tightly, but I could feel her staring at me.

"What, Hecuba?" I cracked one of my eyes open.

Her tall ears laid back against her head and she whined. *"You were too harsh,"* she might have said, had she been able to speak.

"The Gorgon is not my responsibility."

Hecuba was my responsibility, as were Galinthias– the polecat snuggled against my pillow– and the rest of my dogs. The only other responsibility I had ever known had grown from a small child to a renowned witch, and she lived her life in Aeaea.

Sadness swirled around inside me like a blight, dark and all consuming. I did not miss Circe. I had done my due diligence; I had raised her, taught her all I knew, and sent her on her way.

She was never mine to keep forever, and I had known that when I agreed to take her in.

I did not need her, or anyone. I had everything that I needed right within arms reach.

With my eyes closed, I inhaled slowly.

I had everything that I needed.

17

2.

The High Priestess

"Enough is enough, Hades."

He sat, tall and rigid, his dark skin and hair made darker by the shadows of his manor, his red eyes glowing in the dim candlelight. His fingers gripped the arms of his throne so tightly his knuckles turned white.

I kept my eyes locked onto his, refusing to be the first to look away. Exhaustion had left me irritable and frayed at the edge of my patience like a rope ready to snap.

"Do not forget, *Witch*, that I allowed you refuge here when all the other Titans were locked away."

Anger bubbled up to my throat at the name he called me. He used it to remind me I was beneath him. Most of the Gods did. But I was not just any Witch, I was a Titan; a beast older than any of the Gods who strode around on their high horses.

"And you," I snapped, "should not forget that the only reason you 'allowed' me refuge was because deep down you knew I could bring all of Olympus down– the Hells and the earth as well– if I so desired!"

Dark tendrils snaked their way up my legs, coiling and rearing back; poised to strike.

Finally, his stare broke from mine as his eyes dropped to the magic swirling around me. He huffed a heavy sigh and shrugged, completely unbothered by my outburst.

"I cannot and *will not* send the Gorgon away, Witch. Perhaps, if you are so tired of her cries, you could try befriending her."

A snarl curled at my lips and pain stung my palms, my nails piercing the calloused skin there.

He was absolutely useless.

I turned on my heel to storm away and my eyes fell on his harlot Nymph. Blonde hair hung in loose waves down her back, a scarlet dress hugging her curves. Her red lips twitched into a sly smile.

"Wipe that smirk away, Minthe, or I shall slice it off your face," I said through gritted teeth as I passed her.

She frowned and folded her arms. The look she shot Hades was pathetic– tears welling in her large, doe eyes. Hells, did I want nothing more than to turn her into a bug and crush her beneath my foot.

"Always a pleasure seeing you," Hades called out as I slammed the door shut behind me.

Iron crunched under my boots when I slipped out into the Underworld. The gray sky that blanketed above was something I had grown accustomed to. The dark, brooding quiet of the lands below brought me more peace than Olympus ever did.

The humans had become far too fickle– far too brazen– over the years for me to be comfortable in the mortal lands. Their pointless drama and petty wars ensured there was rarely any silence to be found. Long dead was their appreciation and reverence for the Gods. They did not care about us any more than we cared about them. They had found new Gods, young and based in love.

We let them have their Gods, it mattered not to us. For in the end, it would be us they would come to. When their souls departed their bodies and their world, they would find themselves carried across Styx to be wandering shades in Hades' ever crumbling realm forever.

That is… Unless the Goddess of Spring finally showed her face.

Most had come to believe she was a failed prophecy from The Fates. They had never been wrong before, but how many years would we have to wait for her?

Not that it mattered to me.

I lifted my palm and power engulfed me, taking me home– to my small hut, tucked in the wastes of the Underworld. When I appeared in the kitchen, the dogs did not even bother raising their heads, save Hecuba. She lurched to her feet and leaned into my legs, her warmth seeping into the cold Hades' manor had stricken me with.

"He refused again today, dear friend."

'Good. You're being unreasonable,' she would have said, if she could have.

I rolled my eyes at the unspoken words dancing across her face and slumped into a chair at the small table. It seemed I was on my own with the Gorgon.

I would have to find some way to make her want to leave on her own.

My gaze drifted to the tea, stagnant and cold in my forgotten cup. How had I gotten to this point? I was feared once; revered and worshipped. When the Gods of Olympus were just babes, I had laughed at the other Titans for their anxieties about what the Gods would do as they grew in age and power.

But there I was, a sorry lump in the Underworld, bowing and scraping after the pompous God who ruled over it.

Women once called out to me, their hearts or bodies– or both– broken and used by awful men. I would rain terror and pain down over the men, twist their bodies into animals. Some time ago I was one of the only Gods who stood up to any of it; who saw more in the mortal women than just objects.

I was feared once.

A beast. A Titan. A God. A High Priestess, doling out punishments and rewards to those who deserved them.

I laid my head on my arms and closed my eyes, sadness and sleep wrapping me in their lonely embrace.

What had I become?

3.

The Fool

A week had passed since my last visit with Hades, and the Gorgon's wails continued– albeit further from my home than before. I had taken to seeking my quiet time in the mortal lands, nestled deep in the woods away from the humans.

There was no silence during this walk, though. Aphrodite had heard of my excursions in the world above and had taken it upon herself to meet with me.

She walked by my side, light pink silk wrapped around her dark skin, and tight ringlets bouncing as she moved. She was not dressed for a stroll through the woods.

"There are too many bugs out here," she whined as she swatted a fly away.

"The bugs are the least of my concern."

She sighed and leaned her shoulder against mine as we walked. A hard wind blew and swept her perfume forcefully up my nose, nearly gagging me.

"Mortals aren't so bad," she said. "Their wars have settled in recent years."

"I care not for spending my time walking amongst those who have shunned us, Aphrodite."

She would never understand. Her entire existence had been tangled in mortal affairs. Her beauty was unmatched, and it made it easy for her to sway the humans to do whatever she wanted.

"Then why have you so stubbornly decided to spend your time here?" Her eyes lit up, excitement brimming them, as she eagerly waited to hear whatever gossip she felt I was holding hostage.

I groaned. She would find out eventually.

"The Gorgon."

Her brows furrowed. "Athena's acolyte?"

I glanced toward her. An acolyte? That information had evaded me. What could her own acolyte have done to anger her so?

I shrugged. "I suppose."

"Oh dear." She paused, rubbing her hands together. "Is she not adjusting well?"

"Of course not. She was turned into a monster and set loose in the Underworld to roam about, sobbing and ruining my days and my nights."

The look that flashed across Aphrodite's face made my heart sink. There were things I had not been privy to.

"Oh. How sad." Her tone had turned cold, and it was aimed at me.

I stopped walking and she turned toward me, her dark eyes searching my face. A huff left my lips.

"Fine. What happened?" I asked.

Aphrodite stayed quiet, a frown on her face– like she was considering whether or not she should tell me.

"She was an avid follower, spent her days teaching Athena's word," she said. "None of that mattered after Poseidon got his grimy hands on her, though. Athena cursed her all the same."

I shook my head. It was no surprise that Poseidon had done something so horrific. He and Zeus were known to be forceful when it came to getting what they wanted, and what they wanted usually involved women.

"He and his brother are absolutely disgusting. Athena is ignorant if she cannot see that."

"Ignorant or complacent, it does not matter. The details of all that happened are not mine to share, but I know she spent nearly one hundred years imprisoned in Olympus."

"A hundred years?" I could not fathom it. "How did she go from there to the Underworld?"

"Hades," Aphrodite said, a fondness coating her voice. "He fought for her freedom, offered her a sanctuary in his realm."

"He always did have a soft spot for those cast aside by the Gods," I said softly.

Perhaps it was kindness, not fear, that drove him to take me in as well.

"The acolyte was lucky Hades has friends in high places, or Zeus may not have been so quick to comply."

I frowned. "Who else was involved?"

Aphrodite paused, chewing her bottom lip. "I'd rather not say. I doubt she would want all of Olympus knowing she undermined Athena.

"Try to be patient with the acolyte," she continued. "She has lived through far more than any human should. She was not born a beast or a God. She was made of clay and bones, just like any other human. You may forget, Hecate, but you held mortals close to your heart once."

Her words were not meant to sting me, but they did, just the same. It was guilt that worked its way up my throat like bile, guilt that I turned and spewed onto the floor of the forest.

I had been a fool for thinking there was some way the Gorgon had deserved her punishment– a fool for thinking any of the Gods would stop at turning her and then releasing her into the Underworld. Of course she had been imprisoned, probably seen just as many horrors in her confinement as she faced at the hands of Poseidon. The Gods, Olympians in particular, were known for their cruel nature when it came to punishments.

While I had been selfish, thinking of my lost sleep and my solitude, she was alone, wandering the wastes after everything she had no doubt gone through.

With me, just there out of reach– the God who had once prided herself in empowering women; the one who boasted the evils of man. I could have been there for her. I could have helped her.

But instead I moaned and groaned over *my* suffering.

Aphrodite placed a hand gently on my back, rubbing small circles. "You could not have known."

I straightened myself, rubbing my mouth on my sleeve. "I should have."

"All you can do is take the knowledge you have now and move forward with it."

I closed my eyes, the warmth from the sun beating down on my face, the sweetness of Aphrodite still clinging to the air around me. A deep, ugly feeling sat heavy in my stomach, weighing me down.

I would have to make things right with the Gorgon.

She had told me her name, but it slipped from my mind. I could not remember it.

I was a fool, indeed.

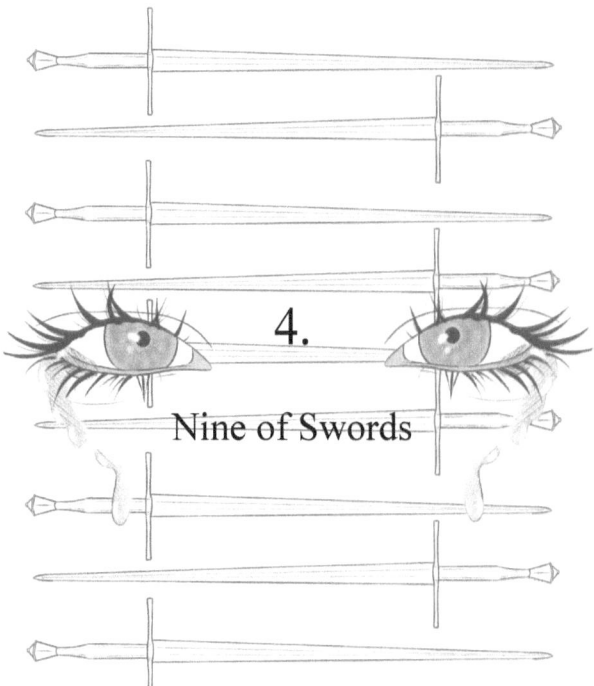

4.

Nine of Swords

I neared The Furies' territory. My heart hammered in my chest as I slowly stepped onward. There were not many things I feared, but The Furies were one of them.

Heartless, rage-filled beasts, twisted and ruined at the hand of Demeter, The Furies destroyed everything they touched. They beat and ripped their way through the mortal lands until they were cast below.

One or two of them I could have taken with ease, but the three of them together? I would leave the fight battered at the very least.

I craned my neck and strained my ears, looking for any sign the Gorgon was nearby, but I could neither see nor hear her. She had not been at her usual place close to my hut either.

"Damned Gorgon."

Of course she would be nowhere to be found as soon as I went looking for her. It was no doubt my own fault I could not find her, after the way I had spoken to her.

A loud screech shattered the stillness of the Underworld and I froze in place. I would never forget that sound.

The Furies.

I wanted to turn and run, to be swallowed by my power and go home. There was nothing to be done, I had tried to find her to make amends.

But...

But the thought of her alone with The Furies kept me from retreating. As deeply as I feared them, how would she have felt being surrounded by them?

She could easily turn them to stone.

But would she?

I groaned and shoved my fear down, marching directly across the invisible line that kept The Furies at bay. The Gorgon was soft, far too kind even after all she had been through. She would not use her cursed eyes on anyone, that much I felt sure about.

It was not long before I found myself moving through a sea of Shades. Their eyes on the ground, and their movements slow. Another feeling slipped from my heart, one I tried to keep tucked out of reach.

Sadness.

This was no way for the Shades to spend their eternity. It was just another reminder of how Hades' vision for the Underworld had fallen short.

I remembered a time, long ago, when he was young and naive. He had wanted to build a place the Shades could revel in for the rest of time. A place where, after all of the turmoil life brought them, they could finally know peace.

But implementing such change takes time and work, and as the years passed I saw the light in his eyes fade– his spark fizzling out. It was a shame. I had once looked at the young God and felt hope for what he could have achieved.

The only thing it had brought me was disappointment, though. He was no different than any of the other Gods. All talk.

I looked around, trying to spot the Gorgon's green hue or her snakes. Once again, I was unsuccessful. My eyes fell on The Furies, instead.

Their leathery wings were spread, their black eyes narrowed, as they screamed and hissed at the Shades who passed. They were nearly identical, each with long, inky hair and tattered dresses draped across their thin bodies. They drew back flails, whipping them toward anyone within reach.

A shiver snaked its way down my spine, a cold sweat forming on my brow. As soon as the fear settled in my stomach, their attention snapped from the Shades to me.

My heart dropped so suddenly I became dizzy. I took a step back and my boot caught on a loose chunk of iron, sending me topping backward onto the hard ground.

I hit the blackened floor of the Underworld and pain shot up my back, the iron scraping my palms. None of that mattered. The Furies were stalking forward, their hollow eyes focused directly on me.

Shades parted for them, leaving a clear path for them to get to me, and I scrambled back. My body shook so violently I struggled to move or stand again, giving me no choice but to scoot away.

I pulled for my power, but the terror that consumed me caused it to slip between my fingers and fade just as fast as I could call it.

"Enough!" I shouted.

The Furies paused, tilting their heads to the side. The Fury standing just to the front let out a loud, shrill cackle.

"Oh? You come to our home and dare to command us?" She laughed again. "We rule this place. It is ours, and all who dwell within it."

I managed to shove myself off the ground and I squared my shoulders, unsure if that was enough to make them believe I was confident.

It became apparent very quickly it was not.

"I've come looking for the Gorgon."

The two further Furies hissed, and the one in front smiled, her sharp teeth gleaming.

"There is no Gorgon here," she said. "For if there was, she would be dead."

I ground my teeth, trying to steady myself before I spoke again. "Very well. Then I shall leave. You three can continue–" I glanced around and then my eyes slid back to them. "Whatever it is you were doing."

The Fury's smile fell away and her wings slowly spread open. "Leaving so soon? Perhaps you could stay a while."

Panic settled over my chest, making it hard to breathe. I took another step back, but before I could do anything else The Furies broke out into a dead run– straight toward me.

In what could only have been instinct, my power erupted out of me, lashing out at Fury and Shade alike, and then it engulfed me. With my senses heightened from fear, the smell of incense that came with my power choked me and burned my eyes, the sting of magic prickling my exposed skin.

When I was finally released from the darkness, I stumbled and fell to my knees. Cold from the iron seeped through my dress and my palms, chilling the sweat that covered my body.

I shook, staring down at the ground, and gasped for air. I hated the way The Furies affected me; hated the slimy feeling their black gaze left me coated in. They were horrid creatures.

My eyes lifted as the sound of rushing water registered, and they fell on Lethe.

My magic had taken me to a place far from The Furies' territory. A place of solitude, for nearly all avoided it, save most of the Shades when they first came to understand they had died.

A place of true peace; of forgetting and being born anew.

I hated Lethe as well as The Furies and the Gods. How could one learn from their mistakes if they did not remember them?

A sigh left my lips and I sat back, staring at the clear river.

"Are you alright?"

My back straightened and my body went rigid, then I relaxed. I knew that voice.

"I've been looking for you all day," I said softly.

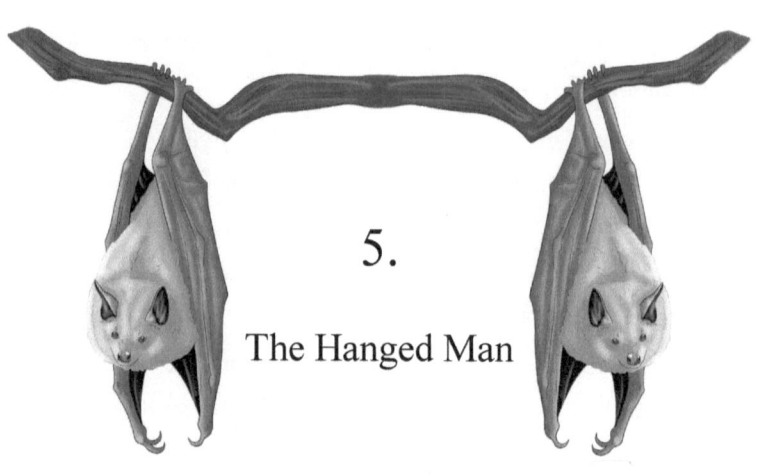

5.

The Hanged Man

Though my eyes stayed on the river Lethe, I could feel the Gorgon's stare. Or perhaps it was the stare of her snakes. Either way, I would not take the chance of being turned to stone.

"You've been quite elusive today," I said when she did not speak.

She stirred to my left, and I had to force myself not to look at her.

"I have been trying to make myself scarce," she said so softly I could barely hear her over the river.

"Even still, this is an odd place to sequester yourself."

Slowly, she inched closer, until she was just feet from me. And then we sat, quietly, side by side, eyes trained on the water. The stillness and silence that hung around us shifted from something uncertain and strange to something comfortable and lulling.

After a long stretch of time she finally spoke, and the words she said shattered a piece of myself I had tried to forget existed.

"I wanted to forget everything. The pain and trauma I have been through," she said, "but also the love and friendships I once knew. It hurts too badly, remembering what I once had; what I'll never have again."

I tried desperately to swallow the large lump in my throat– to ward off the tears stinging my eyes.

But I could not.

The tears slid down my cheeks silently while my mind drifted to Circe. There was no denying it in that moment, no tucking it away or avoiding it. I missed the young Goddess terribly. How could I not? She had been placed in my arms as a babe, and I had raised her as my own. She had spent years in my home, learning dark magic and the ways of the world.

"We cannot forget those we have loved." My voice came out strangled and weak. "It would be a terrible disservice to them."

Once more, her stare bored into me. I kept my face straight, though I longed for nothing more than to look at her. I wanted her to see me, to see my sadness, and to know she was not alone.

"I suppose you are right." She pulled her knees up to her chest and wrapped her arms around her legs. "I know you do not care for me, but I beg you to stay here with me a while. I cannot bear to be alone."

I closed my eyes and breathed in. Her scent wrapped itself around me, a familiar smell. It was Sideritis and fresh spring grass. How I had missed it before, I could not have said.

"I misjudged you, Gorgon. I am deeply sorry for the way I spoke to you."

"Medusa," she whispered.

I cringed and nodded. "Medusa. I am so sorry."

"I do not blame you for lashing out, I might have done the same."

I huffed a laugh. "Somehow, I highly doubt that."

"Well... Perhaps not."

A smile spread across my face, and the sadness that had filled me so wholly just moments before ebbed away. It was not gone, by any means, but calmed and sleeping.

"If you can– I would like to hear what happened to you."

She stiffened beside me, obviously caught off guard by my request. Still, she told me her tale.

I listened quietly, watching the current in front of us, as she recounted her life before it was poisoned. She told me of her friends and family, her time as an acolyte for Athena, her studies. She spared no gory detail as she walked me through the brutal rape she had endured at Poseidon's hands.

She told me how she prayed for Athena's forgiveness for what happened– though it was far from her fault. Athena was less than understanding. Spoiled, she had called her. Ruined and tainted. Hearing Medusa say such things turned my stomach.

Then she told me of her imprisonment, and the pain she suffered there. Athena had snuck into the dungeon, insistent on testing how well she had cursed her. She wanted to make sure her eyes would truly turn someone to stone.

She hesitated, but then recounted the times Poseidon had come to her in the dungeon, sneering and telling her how horrid and destroyed she was. Telling her how he missed the beauty she once held.

And finally, the day Hermes had come to her and announced she was being set free– the day Hades had fought for her– and her travel to the Underworld.

By the time she finished, fresh tears streamed down my face. It was nothing short of a miracle her mortal mind had gone through so much and stayed intact. Because, as Aphrodite had reminded me, regardless of her physical body… She was a human woman.

And that fact had become painfully obvious as she sat next to me.

"You have suffered more than any person ever should, and you did not even deserve it."

"I should have been more modest around him." Her voice was disconnected and distant, as though she was used to dissociating from her body.

The shock of her words caused me to turn without thinking, and my eyes fell on her just in time to see her own squeeze shut. I took her cheeks in my hands. My touch made her tense, and she sat frozen as I studied her face.

"Nothing that happened to you was your fault, Medusa. You could have been covered from head to toe, kept your eyes on the ground, and it would not have made a difference. Gods are terrible. They are no different than men.

"Poseidon was cruel, and unfortunately that is not unlike him. But the cruelty of others does not rest on your shoulders– it is not on you to take the blame for it."

35

She leaned forward, resting her forehead against my collarbone, and her shoulders shook softly as she wept into my dress. I kept my palms flat on the iron ground as she cried into me, fearing I would startle her again if I embraced her.

Eventually her cries slowed to a stop. "Thank you, Goddess," she said between sniffling.

It had been a long time since anyone had called me a Goddess. "Hecate," I said. "You can call me Hecate."

"Hecate," she echoed.

When my name slipped from her lips, there was a tug in my chest– like a string pulled taut– and a whisper carried softly in the air. The voices that reached my ear were so quiet, I thought for a moment I had imagined it. It was another tongue, far older than I had heard in a long time. A language so ancient, most that still roamed the earth had never heard it; a language that predated even the Titans.

I knew deep down who it was, though I would never have admitted it then.

It was The Fates, weaving and knotting my future.

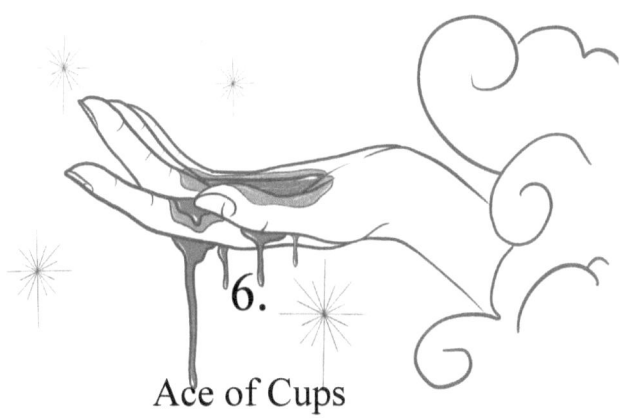

6.

Ace of Cups

I could not have said how long we sat at the water's edge. It felt like days, but then as if no time had passed at all. The rushing sound of the river settled us, as though it were washing all of our troubles away with its current.

"Come back to my home for a while," I said at last. "I can find you something fresh to wear and some food for your belly."

"I could not impose on you in such a way," she said softly.

"Nonsense. I insist. It is the least I could do after being so harsh with you before." The guilt of it all would have eaten away at me from the inside if I did not make up for what I had said to her, and the way I had behaved.

I could tell by her fidgeting, and the restlessness of her snakes, she was hesitant to come with me. It was understandable, after everything she had been through.

"Very well. If you are certain it would not be a bother to you."

"Not at all." I stood, brushing bits of iron from my dress skirt, and then offered her my hand. Her snakes' eyes darted from my face to my hand, then back again. "I will not bite."

I could have sworn a small smile tugged at her lips as she cautiously slipped her hand into mine. I pulled her to her feet, and lifted my other hand to draw out my power to take us back to my home, and she ripped herself from my grasp.

"No," she said, taking a hurried step back. "No, I'd prefer to walk there." Her tone was still polite, but the panic caused her voice to tremble.

I tilted my head and reached for her again. "Don't be ridiculous, this will take just seconds. The walk would be far more trouble than it is worth."

She did not reach out for me again. Instead, she retreated another step. "Travel that way if you must, but I shall walk."

It hit me then, why she would not accept my offer. She had been at the mercy of many Gods and their powers. I could not blame her for the fear and suspicions she felt, allowing herself to once again be subjected to it.

Still... Walking such a distance was completely unnecessary.

I stepped toward her slowly, trying not to scare her off. "I promise you, Medusa, I will only take us to the cabin. I will do nothing else."

Her eyes were squeezed tightly shut, and her snakes bobbed and weaved, eyeing me intensely. "Nothing else?" she whispered.

"No," I said softly. "Nothing else."

She reached out and her fingers slid back into mine. "Alright."

"Alright," I echoed.

I lifted my hand more slowly, drew at my power in a gentler way, coaxing it forward. The darkness that swirled around us was cool. It engulfed us, sending us back to the small hut that was tucked deep into the wastes of the Underworld.

We appeared outside the door, our feet planted on the cold iron, and I looked up at her. Her lips were pulled into a tight line, and her face had gone pale– like she might empty her stomach.

I let go of her and took a step back. "Are you well?"

"Fine," she choked out. "I'll be fine."

As I reached for the door, a nervousness stirred around inside of me; something I had not experienced in a very long time. It was a rare occurrence– visitors– and they usually brought some sort of trouble with them.

"I have dogs," I said suddenly.

Medusa smiled, her face relaxing. "I won't turn them to stone."

A flush spread across my cheeks. "No! I did not mean to insinuate that. I only wanted to warn you. They are rather rude."

"I've always liked dogs– they will be no bother at all."

I nodded, then pushed the door open. "Very well."

Just as I expected, the dogs crowded us at the door, shoving their long noses against her, smelling and searching for affection. They paid no mind to her condition, or the snakes atop her head.

My eyes caught on movement across the room.

Hecuba.

She stared at me, her brown eyes soft, her ears relaxed. Her tail thumped against the floorboards.

Finally, she seemed to say.

I shooed the dogs away, clearing a path for Medusa, and took her hand, guiding her through my home to the long cushioned seat in the sitting room.

"Rest here, I'll fetch us some tea."

She lowered herself down and nodded. "Of course. Thank you."

I left her surrounded by the dogs and made my way to my bedroom. I dug through a large basket, looking for a dress she could wear. Something not completely covered in dog hair, which was impossible, as it turned out. I went to the kitchen next to make tea. It took me no time at all, with my magic, to heat the water and steep the tea. Still, when I returned, Medusa had curled into the pillows and drifted off to sleep.

My eyes stayed glued to her as I approached and sat the cup down on the small, rickety table, the dress clenched in my other hand. I took a seat at her side, and stole the chance to really look at her.

There was something peaceful in the way she slept; something nearly divine blanketing her soft features. Long, dark lashes fluttered against her cheeks and her chest rose and fell in a steady rhythm.

It was a travesty– what Athena had done to her.

Her beauty before the transformation might have put Aphrodite to shame, though I'd never dare say so aloud.

My eyes flicked to the tangle of snakes atop her head.

No. The curse Athena had placed on her did not take from her beauty in the slightest. If anything, the hues of green and sheen from the scales complimented her.

The snakes swiveled their heads to look at me and I averted my gaze to a small crack in the wall.

"Hideous, aren't I?" Medusa asked quietly.

It was so hard to keep myself from looking at her that it physically pained me.

"Not at all." How long had the crack been there? Had I just never noticed it?

"You do not have to lie," she whispered.

Before I realized my mistake, I had whirled toward her and was staring her straight in the face. As if she expected it, her eyes were shut, but her snakes stared at me intensely.

"It is unnerving," I said at last, "the way your serpent friends look at me."

Her lips parted and a laugh slipped from them– the most beautiful sound I had ever heard. It was soft and melodic. Had I not known better, I would have thought her a siren, not a Gorgon.

"They are my eyes," she said. "I often fear even opening my own, so they see for me."

I glanced from her face up to the snakes. I should have realized sooner. Embarrassment caused my face to heat, and my eyes to drift back to the damned crack in my wall. It *had* been rather drafty lately.

"Convenient," I mumbled. "That must be helpful for you."

"It is. It took a while to get used to it, but I enjoy them now."

I looked at her, then the snakes. "Have you named them?"

She chuckled, shaking her head. "No, I suppose I have not. They are so deeply a part of me, I guess I do not think of them as any different. Have you named all of your dogs?"

"Of course, I have. I don't expect you to remember all of them, though." I brushed my fingers through shaggy black fur. "This is Hecuba. She has been by my side for many years, begrudgingly enduring my rather tumultuous life."

Hecuba flashed me a rather impatient look as if to say I was speaking utter nonsense.

I motioned to one of the larger brown dogs, whose nose was particularly prominent. "That is Atalo, he refuses to stop begging for food, no matter how much I fuss over it.

"Cathe and Castor." I motioned to a pair that were nearly identical, except for a small brown patch near Castor's left eye. "Echo, Delphi, Kyrie, Stavros, and—" I pointed at a smaller dog, whose build was much the same as the larger ones, "that is Biscuit. He's the youngest, and has far less intelligence than the others, but I am hopeful he will learn with time."

Medusa smiled, watching as I listed all of the dogs by name, and I wondered if she would truly remember them, or if she even cared at all.

"They are all beautiful, and very sweet natured, it seems."

"I will not keep a dog that has a poor temperament. I had one once, and he nearly destroyed my entire home."

Her face fell. "What did you do to him?"

I frowned. "I found him a better suited home. He lives with Hades now."

"He has a dog?"

I shrugged. "In a manner of speaking."

I was not sure if Cerberus would be better considered a beast than a dog, but it was too much to go into with Medusa.

She pushed herself up, turning to the tea I had placed on the table. "That smells lovely."

"It's Shepherd's tea– made from an herb in the mountains of Greece. It is quite bitter." I was rambling.

"I'm familiar," she said. "We drank it often… before."

I fought the urge to cringe. What a dreadful reminder. Perhaps I would have been better off forgoing the tea entirely.

She reached out and took the cup in her hands, bringing it to her nose to breathe the tea in. "It has been so long since I've had this."

We sat in silence, drinking our tea. When she finished, she placed the cup down. "Thank you. I appreciate what you've done for me."

"It was nothing at all. You have no reason to thank me."

Not yet, at least. Perhaps, if I could convince the King of the Underworld, *then* she could thank me.

"It was not nothing. It was very kind of you, and kindness should be recognized. There is not enough of it in this world."

I hummed. "That is very true. It seems the longer life carries on, the harsher the world becomes. Both in regard to humans and the Gods."

"People are jaded to the beauties of the world and its inhabitants," she said quietly. "We take for granted the things we have at our disposal."

Again, I nearly cringed. If there was anyone who had learned not to take things for granted, it would be her. She had lost everything she held dear to her.

"Indeed. Perhaps we will see a day where that is not true." Though, I highly doubted it. "I hate to bring you here and leave you," I said, pushing myself up to my feet. "But I do have somewhere I need to be; things to tend to."

Her head tilted to the side. "Of course, I'm sorry if I was a bother. I can leave–"

"No," I interrupted. "You do not have to leave. Stay here, I'll be back soon enough."

"I don't want to intrude," she said.

"Nonesense. I'm not going to have you wandering around the Underworld, so that I have to track you down again. I'll leave your change of clothes here, but please, rest, and help yourself to more tea, if you wish. I will be back as quickly as I can."

She fidgeted with the skirt of her dress. "If you're sure."

I reached out and patted her arm. "I am."

Darkness swallowed me, leaving Medusa alone in my home with all of the animals. She could not stay there indefinitely, which was the very reason for my excursion.

I was going to visit with Hades.

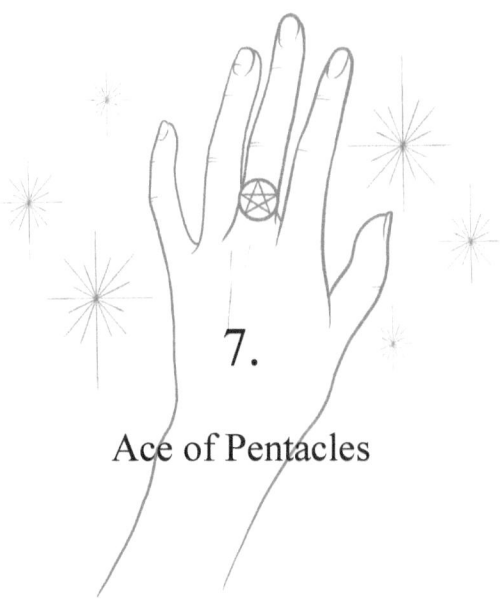

7.

Ace of Pentacles

Patience was never my strong suit, and it was painfully obvious as I sat in Hades' overly extravagant sitting room, waiting for him. It was so quiet you could have heard a pin drop.

Silence was something I usually enjoyed; I once found it comforting, but it was suddenly maddening. Surely he was keeping me waiting to punish me for my behavior during our last meeting.

My fingers absentmindedly drummed along the wooden arm of my seat, the steady rhythm calming my frustration only slightly. The God of the Dead was very quickly becoming less of an indifference to me and more of a bother.

Right as I made to push myself up from the seat, deciding I would rather leave and handle things on my own, he swung the door open and stepped inside.

The lack of urgency in his steps sent a wave of anger blasting through me, and before I could stop myself, I lashed out.

"It took you long enough! That Nymph of yours must be keeping you busy."

His steps halted, and his red eyes flicked to me. I could see unspoken words flitting across his face– a spark of anger, a drop of resentment, and a pinch of embarrassment. That was exactly what I wanted– to strike a nerve.

Once more, he broke eye contact first. It brought me a sick thrill to watch him refrain from engaging with me.

The feeling dropped all at once like a heavy stone, as I remembered I had come to request his approval.

"What do you want, Witch?" He slumped down in his chair, looking like anything but the king that he was.

"I've come to get your authorization to build a home here in the Underworld for Medusa."

He paused, looking at me as though I had grown a second head. "For whom?"

"Medusa," I repeated. When he did not respond, I continued. "The Gorgon you brought here."

His brows rose. "I take it you have moved past your hatred of the Gorgon, then?"

I frowned. "I never hated her."

"Could have fooled me."

We sat, staring at each other as silence stretched between us, then it was my turn to avert my gaze.

"I did not hate her, I was simply tired of her weeping," I said.

He hummed. "And now you wish to build her a home here?"

"Well, she needs somewhere to sleep!" I snapped.

I half expected him to argue, but instead, he nodded. "Very well. I see no problem with that. I only ask that you keep her far enough out that she does not accidentally turn someone to stone."

"She's not going to turn someone to–"

"That is my condition," he interrupted.

I could have blasted him right off of his seat at that moment. Or turned him into a toad.

Instead, I breathed in deeply and tried to calm myself. He had agreed, and arguing with him would only put me at risk of him rescinding his consent on me making her a home at all.

"Fine." My tone was cold. Apparently I was unable to feign subservience in any way. "Her home will be away from the *heavy traffic* you have here."

A muscle in his jaw ticked. It was a fine line I was dancing on– one between grinding his nerves and throwing him into complete rage. I had to admit, though, he had far more patience than I would have, if the roles had been reversed.

Still, it seemed he was making a habit of being an obstacle in my way, regardless of what it was I wanted.

I bowed my head slightly, and turned to leave, but I stopped when he called out.

"Witch!" When I turned back to him, he had a somber expression. "Careful how close you allow yourself to get with her. Word travels, even here, and Athena may find it to be an insult given your... past quarrels."

Athena. I had tried to avoid her after I had taken Hecuba. Not that I could not beat her down on a fair playing field, but she was sneaky and sly. She prided herself on cunning, but she was nothing more than a cheat.

"I'll deal with Athena if it comes to that."

He shook his head. "I have enough to deal with, without petty drama such as this."

Petty drama.

"Fucking Gods," I muttered.

And then I was swallowed by bitter and seething magic.

8.

The Magician

The sun beat down on me, its warmth harsh and suffocating, though the crisp spring air cooled my skin. My walk through the mortal lands was made with light steps, my mood far more bright than it had been just weeks prior.

I spent nearly every day with Medusa. Either with her at my home, or I at her's. Never had I seen so much joy on someone's face without seeing their eyes as I did when I presented her new home to her. It had taken me the entire rest of the day to construct the house, even with my magic, and it had left me drained and sweating by the time I finished.

I was sure it was worth it, though. She was a kind soul, soft and nurturing. The dogs loved her– the polecat, too. Creating her a safe place to live had stirred a feeling of usefulness inside of me I had not felt in a long while.

My eyes drifted across trees and bushes. Spring was the best time for harvesting herbs, right as the new stalks and blooms sprouted from the renewed earth, before the heat of summer strangled the potency out of them.

I would never admit how much I loved the spring, it uncovered a side of me I did not wish to share with anyone. It was a peaceful and private time, one meant only for my eyes.

Several stalks of wild foxglove caught my attention and I paused. When I reached out and plucked one free from the earth, memories flooded me.

At one time I had shared my sacred peace with Circe. Hours upon hours spent picking and gathering, instilling all of my boundless knowledge onto her.

She had been no older than nine or ten, a fledging; a clean slate for me to craft into whatever I wanted. I quickly learned she was a bright child, and the knowledge of toxins and herbs came naturally to her, as did the same dark magic that coursed through my veins.

I turned the foxglove over in my hands, running my thumb against the soft petals.

Hells, how I wished I had not taken my time with her for granted. How I wished I had been more patient and enjoyed her for who she was, and not been so focused on who I wanted her to become.

I shoved the flowers into my satchel roughly, not caring if the blooms were damaged before I got them home. They would be dried and ground into powder anyway.

And there was no reason to dwell on my past mistakes. What was done, was done. Circe's childhood years were long gone, and going over all the things I could have done differently would change nothing.

"What a sight! Picking flowers, Hecate?"

I whirled around, anger contorting my face. I did not need to see him to know who was taunting me. His voice had grated on my nerves and stole my peace for hundreds of years.

"What do you want, Hermes?"

Red hair and hazel eyes gleamed under the light of the sun. He grinned, his expression akin to a cat staring at a mouse. "Must I always want something?"

"Yes." Because that's just how he was.

He slinked closer and I squared my shoulders. With his eyes locked onto mine and his face far too close to my own, he slipped his grubby fingers into my bag and pulled out a stalk of foxglove.

I could have shoved the damned thing right down his throat, and Hells, was it tempting. However, something in the way he looked at me told me he was there on business, not just to torment me. He was, after all, a messenger of the Gods. It brought me great joy to know he was tasked to run errands for the others.

He probably hated it.

"You're being summoned," he said, waving the flowers in my face. There was a gleam in his eyes that filled me with dread.

"If Hades–"

"No, no!" He popped me on the nose with the foxglove, and I snatched it from him. "Not Hades. You're needed in Olympus."

Fuck.

That couldn't be good.

"Why?"

He shrugged. "As if I'm privy to the details."

I felt sure he was, but arguing with him was like arguing with a wall. It would serve me better to simply comply with his game and make my way to Olympus.

"Who has summoned me?"

"Who do you think?"

I hesitated. There were several Gods I could imagine might summon me, and most of them were for rather unpleasant matters.

When I did not answer, he continued. "I believe it is the beloved daughter of Zeus."

Fuck.

"You believe?"

His grin spread to a smile. "I thought that might soften the blow."

I truly did not understand how Hermes had managed to avoid being locked away for his antics.

Black magic pulsed through my veins and I raised my hands, giving way to the rippling power, clearing it a path. There was no point in prolonging the inevitable.

"Wait!"

I turned. "What?" I snapped.

"She's very upset. You should tread carefully today." His smile was bright, his arms folded across his chest. He was enjoying every bit of my frustration.

He had some nerve.

I shrugged. "I am fully capable of dealing with her."

"I think you'll arrive to find her in rare form," he said.

Rare form? Zeus' golden child stayed in that state. It could hardly be considered rare.

"You should worry about yourself, Hermes. I've lived a long time and crossed beings far worse than Athena."

As darkness consumed me, I caught a glimpse of something in his face that made my confidence falter.

What the Hells was I about to walk into?

9.

Five of Swords

Cobbled streets, laden in gold, glinted in the unnatural light of Olympus. Pristine temples and homes with intricate pillars had been erected since my last visit to the land of the Gods. There were far fewer trees, though the ones who still stood were tall and sturdy. My heart broke at the sight of it all. The trees had been on the sacred mountain long before the Gods made it their home, before they cast the Titans out and conquered the land.

It was a pity and a shame. They had desecrated a once perfect haven in the name of vanity and pride.

But that was no longer my problem. Olympus had not been mine in many years.

I marched through the empty streets, the darkness of my wardrobe and hair like a stain on the starkness of the city. I was going straight to the smaller temples, just outside of Zeus' grounds. There were two Gods never permitted to be too far from Zeus and Hera.

Hera's pride and joy, Hephaestus, and Zeus' favorite daughter, Athena. His favorite child, if I were to be honest. I was never sure he even liked any of the others.

When the two Gods were young, I felt pity for them. Living under the constant watchful eyes of their parents was certainly no easy upbringing.

My sympathy for them quickly fled, though. Hephaestus was soft, unlike the metal he worked and shaped. He bent to Hera's will without hesitation.

And Athena... Athena was cold and calculated. She used anything she could to gain the upper hand on those weaker than her, including her father's favor. The last of my pity for her died the day she had Odysseus cast Hecuba into the sea.

The two of us had not seen eye to eye since.

As I approached her temple, I paused. It was a smaller version of Zeus'. White marble pillars, and golden art scrawled along the outer walls. In the front was a large statue of– of course– Athena herself.

The prideful nature of the statue made me nauseous.

I pushed the door of the temple open and stepped inside. While the outside of the building mirrored a place of worship, the inside could not have been further from it. The Naos had been cleared of its seats and altars and filled with training dummies and weapons. Swords and spears lined the walls and cluttered the racks. Shields were strewn haphazardly across the floor.

A wave of disgust rolled through me at the sight of it. The temples in Olympus had always sickened me– it was a mockery of the humans who worshiped the Gods. But to defile a Naos in such a crude manner was too much.

Not that it would ever be used as it should.

Footsteps echoed through the mostly empty dwelling, drawing my attention to Athena as she crossed from the hall beyond into the room. To my surprise she did not wear her armor or helm, but instead, an ivory chiton. Blonde hair, slightly brighter than her mother's, cascaded, unbound, down her back.

She looked nothing like her father, save her eyes. They held swirling gray storm clouds, bright and angry.

"I didn't think you would come," she said.

I shrugged. She thought to intimidate me, but she was young and far more naive than she gave herself credit for. The Gods had called me a witch for so long they forgot the ancient magic running through my veins. I was more than any witch or God that had come after me. I was more than the other Titans before me.

"I did not realize the invitation was optional, or I would have declined."

She smirked, and strode closer. I did not miss her eyes flicking to the spear displayed on the wall as she passed it. Whether she was just admiring it or planned to use it, I was unsure. Though, the uncertainty would fall away soon enough.

"You misunderstand, Witch. My summon was not optional– I merely thought you a coward."

I bit the inside of my cheek, fighting to hold my tongue. She just wanted to goad me, to anger me. I would not allow myself to fall into whatever trap she was setting for me.

"How many years have you spent hiding, now?" she continued. "I almost forgot what you looked like. I would have sworn you were an old woman."

I folded my arms. "Did you bring me here to taunt me, Athena, or is there something else?"

She smiled. "I'm not taunting you. Just catching up."

"I have no desire to catch up with you," I snapped. "If that is all you want, I'll be leaving."

I turned on my heel to leave, coaxing my magic to the surface. As it welled and slipped free, Athena spoke again– cutting off my magic and causing my body to freeze.

"Tell your whore I said hello."

I whirled, my eyes burning, and when the words left my lips they echoed as a monstrous symphony. "You lost your right to speak of Medusa the day you cast her aside. I'll not stand here and listen to you sully her name."

Athena's arms stretched open. "I cannot sully her. She did that to herself, already."

Before I knew what was happening, my magic erupted, ripping itself free of its restraints, and blasted toward her. Her arms opened and she muttered something under her breath. I did not hear what she said, but I knew her words were not meant for me. Her spear rattled from its place on the wall and the shield from its place on the floor. They both flew to her hands.

She deflected my blow and sent it blasting into a pile of worn blades.

"Poseidon's shortcomings are not her reflection!" I sent another wave of dark fire at her and she shielded herself from it once more.

"Now," she said, her voice full of satisfaction, "if you want a fight, all you have to do is ask."

Tendrils of dark power wrapped themselves around my arms, as my anger for Athena's outrageous remarks, and Poseidon's disgusting behavior settled over me.

"Do not fool yourself, child. It would be no fight at all."

She laughed, opening her arms once more. "Drop your magic, then. Beat me fair and square."

As if I were stupid enough to drop my most likely chance to protect myself.

"What are you getting out of this, Athena? I have done nothing to you."

She snarled. "Yet, you have. The Gorgon should not be enjoying her life or making friends. She should be punished."

My eyes dipped to Athena's fist, tightened around her spear, then back up to her face. "She has been punished enough."

"I disagree."

I shook my head. "I don't understand how you can be so cruel, Athena. You know she did nothing wrong."

The smirk on Athena's face might have been enough to send me over the edge, but like her father, she had to have the last word.

"You always did have a weakness for whores and charlatans, didn't you?"

Power swelled so suddenly I thought it might destroy me. "You pious little brat."

And then every drop of anger flooded into the dark magic swirling around me and lashed out at Athena.

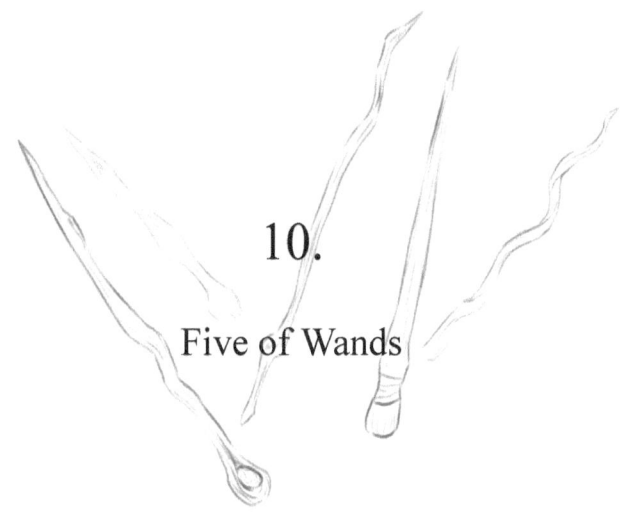

10.

Five of Wands

Something dark and ancient seeped its way into my magic. It crept from the very depths of the Chaos from which we were all born. It sang to my blood as it filled me and warped the tendrils that struck at Athena. A slimy residue was left on my soul– one I feared I might never be rid of.

Even as I used that darkness, melded it with my own, I worried I would be tainted by it forever.

It didn't stop me from clawing for it, though. I would use whatever I had at my disposal to make sure Athena thought twice about speaking ill of Medusa again. I would remind her exactly what I was– and what I was capable of.

Power cracked and whistled through the air. It found its mark, slamming into Athena, knocking her flat on her back and tearing her flesh open. Her skin charred and darkened at the site of the wound, blood dripping to the floor. Whatever I had tapped into was slowing her healing.

Despite what I had done to her, she shoved herself back up to her feet.

"Pick up a sword and fight me, Witch!" Athena yelled.

I let my magic build around me again, the same oily substance from Chaos soiling it. "Scared of my power, Athena?"

Her face stayed neutral, but her fingers tightened around her spear. "If you win, I'll never speak of the Gorgon again. And if I win–"

"You won't."

"If I win, you send her back to me to serve the rest of her punishment."

I sent another whip of magic at her, but she deflected it with her shield.

"She is not some object to be bartered!" I seethed.

Athena smiled, adjusting her grip on the spear. "Perhaps I'll just go take her, then?"

Red filled my vision as anger blasted through me. I threw my hand toward her and purple flames erupted from my palm. Athena held her shield up and fire met metal. It turned white hot and she yelled out, tossing it to the floor. Her face was contorted with rage, the storms in her eyes growing restless.

"You'll not lay a finger on her!" I yelled.

"Pick up a sword, then!" Athena said. "Fight me fair and square."

There was a tightness in my chest– a tug– as I stared into the storms that swirled in Athena's eyes. My options were clear; duel Athena and win or risk her taking Medusa. They weren't choices, not really. I could not take any chances of Medusa ending up at the mercy of Athena.

I would not waste anymore time standing by while women were abused. Long ago it was my job to keep them safe, to punish those who harmed them… and I had somehow lost that part of myself over the years.

No longer.

My hands dropped to my sides and I turned from Athena. I felt her eyes on my back as I walked over to a table cluttered with swords and daggers.

A blade was something I had never been adept with, but there was no other option for me. I would have to best Athena at her own game.

I reached out and grabbed a short sword. My fingers tightened around the grip and I lifted it. The weight of it was foreign, and doubt tried to sneak in, but I shook it off. Failure was not an option.

With the sword raised, I turned to Athena and gave her a curt nod. "A fair fight, then."

She smiled. "A fair fight."

In a blink, she was running full speed toward me, her spear drawn back. I barely had time to raise the sword as she stabbed at me. Metal clashed against metal, the sound ringing in my ears. Before I realized what was happening, a new shield was flying through the air and into her hand. She slammed it against me and my body fought to keep me upright, my feet struggling to stay on the floor.

The spear cut through the air at me again, aimed right at my chest. The muscle in my arm cramped as I swung the sword up, knocking her spear back. The sudden, jarring movement caused me to stumble and fall. Pain shot through me, like a jolt of lightning down my spine.

Athena moved before I had time to realize what she was doing.

She brought the spear down on me, and I rolled out of the way, scrambling up to my feet behind her. I swung the heavy blade at her. She turned, but not fast enough. The sword sliced her upper arm, splattering blood across the marble floor of the temple, but Athena did not even react. She spun toward me, smashing her shield into my chest.

"Is she worth it?" Athena said. "You're putting quite the effort in for someone who has been soiled and ruined. Perhaps that's how you like them?"

Athena's words did not reach me; I knew she was trying to cloud my mind so I could not think well enough to fight. I shifted to the side, pushing her shield down and struck her with the pommel of the sword. It made contact with her nose, and again, blood sprayed.

She did cry out that time, though.

I had no time to celebrate my hit before she was stabbing at me with her spear again. It sliced down at my leg and– had I not moved just enough– it would have impaled me. Her shield smashed into my face, cracking my nose just as I had hers.

"Poseidon said she was dripping by the time he was done with her. I wonder, do you get her just as wet?"

Between the sharp pain in my face, the ringing in my ears, and the taunting, Athena had succeeded. I could no longer think straight at all.

The sword swung on its own; it did not need me. It clashed into her shield and spear, sliced into her skin. The clang of metal and both of our screams rang out.

Swipe after swipe I made caused Athena to retreat. She was using her shield far more than her spear, and panic settled over her gray eyes.

I was winning.

Athena muttered under her breath and out of nowhere, I was struck in the back of the head with a shield. Pain blasted through me, and my vision went white. Then Athena's foot slammed into my chest, knocking me flat on my back. When I opened my eyes, her spear was pointed at my throat.

"That's enough!"

We both turned. Ares stormed into the temple, his blonde hair brushed back, and a rugged beard covering his square jaw. A golden chest plate gleamed in the light spilling in through the windows, and a red cape billowed behind him. His blue eyes met mine and relief washed over me.

I looked back up at Athena and snarled. "You cheated!"

She spit blood onto the floor next to me. "I still won."

"You said a fair fight," I said, pushing myself to my feet.

She smiled, her face resembling her father's. "All is fair in battle, Witch."

Magic ripped free and I sent another blast of fire toward her. She screamed, throwing her shield up.

"Enough! Both of you!" Ares yelled. "This is over."

My fists balled at my sides. I should have known Athena would never fight fair, should have known she would use her words to blind me enough that she could cheat.

She threw her shield and spear down, raising her hands. "Fine. Keep your Gorgon. Just remember– you claim to view her as more than an object, but you bartered her life to prove a point to me just now. You're no better than Poseidon."

All of the air fled from my lungs, leaving me broken and angry, still.

Ares rushed to my side. No doubt he thought he would have to drag me out of the temple. And he would have, if I had tried to stay. But I had no intention of continuing my fight with Athena.

There was someone else who deserved just as much of my anger, if not more.

And he was about to be at the receiving end of it.

11.

Strength

"Hecate, wait!"

I ignored Ares' pleas from behind me. My eyes were trained ahead and my steps were sure. Nothing Ares could say or do would change my mind.

I was going to Poseidon.

"Would you stop?" Ares grabbed my arm and spun me around to face him. "You are covered in blood and you aren't thinking straight."

"I assure you, I am thinking just fine!" I said, snatching my arm free.

We stared at each other, my chest rising and falling with my rapid breaths. His eyes searched my face, looking for–

I could not be sure what.

"Please tell me you are not about to do what I think you are."

"I am!" I snapped. "I should have done it a long time ago."

His face fell and he shook his head. "You are going to get yourself in a lot of trouble."

I knew he said it because he cared. Ares was a warrior; one of the strongest Gods I had ever met, but he was also one of the kindest.

Of course, he didn't want anyone else to know that.

I leaned in, scowling. "I'd like to see Zeus try to stop me."

His hand found my cheek. "He will. You might not be as lucky as you were the first time you took a stand against him."

Flashes of war long since passed flooded my mind. Titans littering the ground of Olympus, their blood feeding the earth. Some shackled and chained– their futures set for Tartarus. Black magic, blasting and burning everything around me. And Zeus– young, full of pride, and a vision for his future. There was real, desperate fear in his eyes that day. That might have been the only time I had ever– or would ever– see it.

I shook my head slowly. "Zeus took Olympus because I let him."

Ares' shoulders drooped, sympathy falling over his face. "Zeus took Olympus because he and the other Gods stood as one. They ambushed the Titans."

We stared at each other in silence. His words struck me through the heart like a dagger, but even I had to admit– they held truth.

My eyes dropped to his chest plate and then I paused. It was polished, gleaming in the glow of the divine light of Olympus around us. His clothes and armor were usually dented and bloody; covered in the evidence of his constant need for battle.

"You look rather dashing today," I said.

He grinned. "Are you trying to woo me, Hecate?"

I scoffed. "Don't flatter yourself." I leaned in, inhaling deeply. A familiar sweetness choked my senses, gagging me, and I pulled away quickly. "Ares!"

He took a hurried step back. "What?"

But I could see in his face he already knew.

"She is betrothed!"

He stilled, his eyes going wide, then he straightened his back. "I love her."

"Hells! You gargantuan fool!" I slammed my palms into his chest plate, shoving him back. "You stand there and speak of the decisions I make. Try to tell *me* how to live? Look at your own choices, Ares, and leave mine alone!"

"You don't understand." He grabbed my hand as I turned to storm off, and pulled me toward him again. "You make your choices based on your pride and guilt. *I love her.* When you fall so deeply it consumes you entirely– then you can judge me. But do not speak to me as if I am some ignorant child! Do not treat me the way everyone else does."

I recoiled, pulling free of his grasp. Anger and hurt filled his blue eyes; his mouth pulled into a tight line.

A sigh left my lips, and I reached out, placing my hand against his cheek. "I do not think you ignorant, Ares. Foolish, perhaps, or blinded by her beauty and honey tongue, but do not mistake the intentions of my words."

He placed his hand atop mine, looking down at me with hope. "She means to be with me. She is trying to find a way to break it to him."

I forced a smile. It was hard to be happy for him. I loved Aphrodite– I always had– but I held much less faith in her promises than Ares did. She was fickle, and I wondered if there was anything, or anyone, who could ever truly satisfy her.

"We've drifted, Ares," I whispered.

He closed his eyes and nodded, and when he opened them his mask of strength was back in place. "I still think this is a bad idea."

"Perhaps you are right, my friend, but I intend to see it through."

He brushed a raven curl behind my ear. "Should I accompany you?"

My brow arched and a grin spread across my face. "I'd think you've enough of your own issues to deal with. I can handle mine on my own."

He took my hands in his and gave them a tight squeeze. It was a shame he so rarely showed that part of himself. I wondered if the other Gods would hold him in a higher esteem if he did not lean so far into his facade of an emotionless warlord.

"May The Fates guide your hand and your fractious temper, then."

I gave him one slight nod and then turned, a fire burning deep in my belly. I had never met The Fates, few had, but I felt sure they would side with me.

They had kept the utmost care of my life string; had cradled it like a babe and ensured my safety. They would not desert me now.

12.

The Chariot

I hadn't intended to make a show of it; a public display, or use him as an example. My intention was to dole my retribution in private. Not that he deserved it. However, Poseidon was not at his temple when I arrived.

Sure, I could have waited, or scoured the oceans in search of him, but if I were to be honest, I was far too eager to wait. I wanted to watch him pay for what he did, and I did not have the patience to wait for it.

So I found myself marching into the temple of Zeus. I had only walked it a handful of times, and it had been many years, but still, the layout was as fresh in my mind as if I had walked it every day.

I passed paintings and sculptures in both his and Hera's likeness, as well as the large peacocks Hera so adored. I found the birds atrocious, myself.

Their courtyard was immaculate, which came as no surprise. Hera took great pride in her gardens and grounds, though it was Rhea, not Hera, who tended to them. I wasn't sure how often Rhea came to Olympus in recent years, but unless she had greatly changed, I assumed it was very infrequent. Not that I could blame her.

When I came to the large, ornate doors, I paused. Doubt trickled into my heart.

I could not help but wonder if Ares was right; if I was marching into the temple with the wrong intentions. Was I really no better than Poseidon?

I thought of Medusa; her gentle smile and meek mannerisms, and my doubt fell flat.

No.

I was not doing it for my pride or my guilt. I was doing it because through everything she endured, no one stood behind her. Not a single person protected her. She– who was innocent to the bone– was left to pay the price of the two cold-hearted Gods who wronged her. Medusa did not deserve that.

The same tightness in my chest I felt before tugged at me again, and before I could second guess myself, I pushed the doors open.

My goal was to demand Zeus to send Hermes to summon Poseidon, but as the doors swung open and my eyes swept across both Zeus and Hera perched on their thrones, I saw my target right amongst them.

He stood near Zeus' throne. The two Gods, both resembling their brother who resided in the lands below, had obviously been

70

engaged in deep conversation. Their faces were serious and a somber aura radiated from them both. Whatever they were discussing, it no longer mattered. I had more important things to address.

"Well," Zeus said. "If it isn't the Witch."

I stepped into the room, not bothering to bow or recite pleasantries. I was not there to fuel their egos. "Zeus. I have made a reputation for myself bringing vengeance for women who have been slighted, have I not?"

His brows furrowed and he exchanged an uneasy glance with Hera. His words came slowly and deliberately. "I suppose so. What matter have you brought before me today?"

As if I were a peasant coming to beg him for some grace on taxes.

"I am not here for you," I said flatly.

"Spit it out, Witch. We do not have all day," Hera said.

Witch. Every time they said it, a fire blazed inside of me, and I came closer to combusting right where I stood.

"I came for payment on an account that happened many years ago with Poseidon."

He spread his arms open wide. "That is absolutely ridiculous! You cannot possibly mean to try and punish me for something I did years–"

Zeus held up his hand and cut Poseidon off. "Sorry, Witch. I'm afraid that will not be taking place. You punish mortals for their wrongdoings– not Gods."

"You misunderstand me, Zeus. I am not asking for your permission."

He straightened on his throne. It was not meant as an insult, but I was sure he took it as one by the look on his face.

71

"Do you mean to say that you plan to go against my word intentionally?"

I arched my brow. "Yes."

He laughed loudly, his voice booming like thunder. "So you come into my temple, covered in blood like you were just slaughtered on a battlefield, and expect to reprimand my brother as if he were some lowly mortal? I think not."

"Who?" Hera asked. "Who have you come on behalf of?"

Zeus whirled to look at her. "Hera, we will not be entertaining this–"

"Medusa."

He looked at me again. "Who?"

"The acolyte," Hera said before I could.

He turned to his wife, brows furrowed. "The acolyte?"

Somehow it only enraged me more that Zeus could not immediately place her. She had not been in the Underworld long.

Hera looked over at him. "The Gorgon we sent below."

Zeus threw his head back and laughed again, but Poseidon had stiffened, his face drained of color.

"You jest!" Zeus said between laughs. "Surely you do not stand before me on behalf of a beast!"

"She is a human woman!" I snapped.

Zeus' laughter died and his face became serious. "Why is this so important to you?"

"Because…" Because?

I could not put it into words.

"Do it."

I whirled to look at Hera. "What?"

"What?" Zeus echoed.

72

Hera leaned forward, her eyes glued to me. "What happened to that poor girl was a tragedy. Your anger is well placed."

Zeus opened his mouth to argue, and Poseiden lifted his arm to call his power forth and flee, but I would not allow it.

I opened my soul to the oily, tainted magic from the depths of Chaos, and I drank it in. It filled me, destroying and rebuilding me from the inside out. My body burned, needle pricks dancing across my skin as I grew old and then young over and over again.

And then it lashed out at Poseidon as a dozen dark tentacles. As soon as they made contact with him, his magic faded and he was at my mercy.

His screams filled the room and blood sprayed the pristine marble walls and floor. I pulled from the Chaos, grasping for as much as it would allow me to take. I did not stop until the Chaos abruptly shut me out and I was left heaving on my knees, gasping for air.

I faintly heard Zeus call for his youngest son, Apollo, to come and heal Poseidon.

But all of my attention was on the God of the Sea as he choked on his own blood, laying helpless on the floor unable to heal.

I was left further soiled by Chaos, some vital part of myself forever changed.

And I promised myself right at that moment…

Medusa would never know what I had done.

13.

The Moon

I was clean when I arrived home again– at least outwardly. All of the blood and grime from my trip to Olympus had been washed away at Ares' temple.

Inside, however, a residue from Chaos clung to me. No amount of scrubbing would rid me of it. Certainly, I knew deep down I should not have allowed myself to use it. Its power was unstable.

I could not find it in myself to regret what I had done, though. Especially as I slipped further into the den and my eyes fell on Medusa.

Hells, she was beautiful. The candles sent a soft light dancing across her scales, making them almost shimmer. She was curled under a small fur cover, sleeping. It was the only time she truly looked peaceful.

I tiptoed over the pile of dogs and knelt beside her. Her snakes rustled and lifted their heads to look at me, and with her eyes still closed, she spoke.

"Sorry for the intrusion."

"Is all well?" I asked.

She stretched out and yawned, and I caught myself smiling.

"I drifted off to sleep at my own home, but I woke from a rather dark dream and I didn't want to be alone. I knocked first, but it appeared you were not home." She sat up, her brows knitted together. "I'm sorry. I should not have come in while you were away."

"Nonsense. You are welcome to come here anytime, whether I am home or not. So long as you are not wailing."

She let out a soft, airy laugh and my chest grew tight. "Of course. No more wailing."

I stood, tossing my satchel of herbs and plants on a small table. "Come, I'll fetch us some tea."

She followed me to the kitchen, as did all of the dogs. Galinthias was curled on the table, her soft stomach exposed. She had been with me a while, but never had I seen her so brazen as to lay where I ate my meals.

"What the Hells are *you* doing?"

Galinthias popped her head up and yawned. To my surprise, she did not scamper away as she usually did when I scolded her, but tucked her head back into her small arm.

"Sorry," Medusa said. "She was trying to sleep on a fur blanket on the floor, but the Castor nearly stepped on her several times, so she had to keep moving. I thought she might rest better if she was up high."

I turned to Medusa and my heart broke. Her face was tight, her lips pulled into a frown. She looked as though she was waiting for me to yell at her.

Honestly, before that day, I might have. But Medusa had suffered enough. I could deal with a weasel sleeping on my table. On a grander scale, it seemed a small thing.

"It's fine," I said. "She deserves sleep just as well as the rest of us."

I reached for the pot of water and lifted my hand to ignite a fire with my magic and I hesitated. My eyes flicked to Hecuba and she shot me a knowing look, then I reached for my kindling and lit a small fire on the stove to heat the water.

"Are you well?" Medusa asked. "You do not usually do it that way."

"It doesn't take that much longer. No point in draining myself." But in truth, I knew she flinched every time I used my magic around her.

Perhaps she would see through my lie, or perhaps not. Either way, I was starting to feel like everything I did would cause her some sort of pain. The way I lived my life would keep her on edge. Could I live with myself, knowing I was bringing her such grief?

"We've been together nearly every day," she said, changing the subject. "Yet, I feel I hardly know you. Do you have friends? Family?"

Her question was asked in innocence, but knowing that did not keep it from stinging. Friends? I wasn't sure I could call anyone that. My relationship with Ares and Aphrodite was pleasant enough– but did that make them my friends?

And family... No, I could not have said that either. As badly as I regretted it, I had raised Circe like a pupil– not a daughter. I had no parents or siblings, either.

I was alone.

I looked at Hecuba again and damned me, if she didn't have sadness in her eyes.

"You have me," she seemed to say.

But she was not a friend or family, not really.

"No."

I could feel Medusa shift behind me, but I kept my attention focused on the water.

Would it ever boil?

"I suppose I don't either," she said quietly. "Everyone I had before is surely long gone."

I closed my eyes. Again, I had slipped into my own pity, forgetting she had been through far worse. Medusa needed to find someone else– I could not be the companion she needed.

"Well," I said, turning toward her. "Maybe I could help you find someone."

Her hands fidgeted in her lap. "I do not think that is a wise idea. I could never live with myself if I hurt someone."

"You've done well with me. I've not turned to stone yet."

She said nothing for what felt like forever, her lips pulled into a tight line.

"Have you grown tired of me?" she asked at last.

No. My eyes searched her face. No, I wasn't sure I would ever grow tired of her. She was everything I wished I could be. Kind, thoughtful, gentle and mild. Yet, somehow unbreakable. I could see myself spending every day with her for the rest of time and never being sick of it.

But how long would it take before I changed her? Before she became dark and cynical? I could not bear the thought of spoiling her good nature.

"Perhaps I have." The words left my lips in a rush, before my aching heart had a chance to swallow them.

She would find someone else– someone far better suited to be her friend.

I heard the water boiling as steam filled the room, but I could not tear my eyes from her back as she walked away without another word. The door creaked open and shut softly behind her as she left my home in silence.

The tightness in my chest returned so suddenly it nearly brought me to my knees, and tears stung my eyes.

I could not bring myself to look at Hecuba. I knew she was also hurt by what I said. She would not understand what I was feeling and what I was doing.

And Medusa... I hoped she never forgave me for what I said. I hoped it hurt her enough to leave me and never look back.

Tears streamed down my face and my legs gave out from under me. I did not understand why my body betrayed me, or why my chest ached so terribly. I had done it for Medusa's own good. It was all for the best.

My pain was so consuming, I barely heard the faint whispers in ancient tongues filling my ears. It did not matter what they were saying– I had made my choice.

Even if I was never the same for it again.

It was for Medusa. Everything that I was doing was for her.

14.

Three of Pentacles

My eyes flew open, my ceiling coming into view. Everything was too quiet. I reached out for Hecuba, but my hand found only the bed beneath it. I sat up and looked around the room. Hecuba was not there at all, nor were the other dogs, or Galinthias.

I threw my covers off and slipped from my bed, throwing a robe over my nightdress, then yanked my door open. The smell of tea and eggs hit me all at once.

"What in the name of the Hells?" I muttered.

I made my way to the kitchen and when I rounded the corner, I paused. Medusa stood at the small stove, fussing over burnt eggs while Hecuba and the other dogs were gathered at her feet, hoping she would drop something. Galinthias was on the table again, sleeping.

My heart skipped at the sight of her. It was a dreadfully unpleasant feeling– one that nearly sent me running from the Underworld entirely.

"Good morning," she said softly, without turning to face me.

"You are not supposed to be here." I had meant for it to come out harsh, to scold her. Yet, instead, my words left my lips almost breathlessly.

It was surprise. She had caught me off guard.

She stilled at my comment, and I thought she would turn and leave again– but she did not.

"Yes, well… I know what you said yesterday, but I thought perhaps you went so long without having someone who cared for you that you did not know how to accept it. Friendship, that is."

I knew her snakes were watching me, but I could not make my mouth close, or stop the welling of tears. The woman before me– the one who had suffered so greatly– she was trying to take care of me; to give me something I never had before.

I did not deserve that, and she deserved better. She needed someone who could care for her in ways I could not.

"No." I walked over and pulled the cups of tea from her hands and set them aside. "No, I do not want your friendship. Go find someone else. Hypnos is very kind– he can be your friend."

Her snakes stared at me, their bodies coiled tightly. They looked less than pleased with me. Medusa stood with her shoulders squared.

"You do not mean that," she said.

"I assure you, I do."

Her brows furrowed. "Then tell me you hate me."

I flinched. Could I go that far for her sake, or was I too selfish?

"Hate is a strong word–"

"If you cannot say it, then you cannot possibly be tired of me."

I crossed my arms. She was persistent, I would give her that. "You cannot know how I feel."

"Can't I?" she pushed. "I was drawn to you. Even before I met you, I was drawn to your home. The Fates have brought me here for a reason, and I think you are that reason."

Hells below, my face grew *warm*.

"I don't know how to be your friend." The admittance stung, and as soon as it left my lips, I regretted it. It seemed I was too selfish to send her away, after all.

She reached out and took my hands into hers. "Then let me teach you. No one should have to go through life alone."

"I may hurt you. My mouth seems to get the better of me most days."

The snakes' eyes dipped to my lips and Medusa smiled. "I am not afraid of your mouth, Hecate."

I found myself inspecting her face, again. Her thick lashes, the soft curve of her nose. And her lips–

I pulled my hands free and took a step back. "Very well. But don't say I did not warn you."

She flashed me a smile and then grabbed the two cups of tea. "Good. Now, let us eat. I'm starving."

I felt quite ravenous myself as I watched her fill the table with the food she had made. She caused me to feel things I had never experienced before.

My eyes slid down her body as she turned from me, and Athena's words echoed in my head.

Perhaps I *was* no better than Poseidon.

15.

Two of Cups

"I've been working on this damned thing for weeks! It's no use– I'll never get it right."

Medusa's snakes peered over at my pathetic excuse for embroidery and she smiled. "I think this one is much better than the last."

"You lie. I can clearly see how horrible this looks."

I did not even understand how she had talked me into attempting such a mundane activity. Hers looked incredible, of course.

"It just takes practice. Here–" She slid closer to me, placing her hand atop mine.

The touch was simple; it was light. Still, it sent my heart sputtering in my chest. I nearly recoiled, and would have abandoned my place on the floor next to her, had I been able to move.

83

She guided my hand through what she called a novice stitch, explaining how and why it should be done just so, but her words were muffled in my ear. Each day it grew increasingly more difficult to focus around her. Every time her skin touched mine, my face grew hot and my heart hammered.

She was a human– one who had suffered at the hands of a God. Thinking of her in such a way made me feel almost as gross as the film left by the power from Chaos that I used. It was wrong of me to let my mind and my eyes wander. She needed friendship, not...

And she surely would never wish to be touched by a God again, not so intimately.

"Hecate?"

My attention snapped up from her lips to her closed eyes. "Yes?"

"You seem lost in thought. Did you hear anything I said?"

My cheeks grew hot, and suddenly her hand on mine was all I could think about.

"I did not," I whispered.

I could not have been sure, but her face seemed to flush. She did not pull away, though. Nor did she put any distance between us, so I told myself I had imagined it.

My thoughts were consumed by the sight of her, the smell, the feel of her skin.

I was no better than a man.

"Are you well?"

"Fine," I quipped.

We sat in silence, neither of us moving a muscle. Then her fingers brushed gently from mine up to my arm. It was like fire dancing across my skin, and it caused my stomach to flip.

"Do you wish to discuss what is on your mind?"

I yanked my arm back and scooted away from her. "No. And I'm tired of embroidering. We should do something else."

"Of course." She paused briefly before adding, "what is it you wish to do?"

My eyes lifted from the floor and met her face. There were a great many things I wished to do, and not a single one of them were appropriate.

"What else did you do in your spare time before?" I asked, changing the subject.

Anything to get my mind from thoughts of my lips and hands roving her body.

She sighed, leaning her back against the wall. "There was not much we were permitted to do as acolytes of the temple. We cleaned, cooked, and prayed. Embroidery was one of the only pleasurable things we were allowed." Her face lit up and she turned to me quickly. "Sometimes, during the spring months, we would gather flowers and braid them into crowns, or weave them in our hair. I miss that."

The joy in her voice at the memory made me glad I was sitting– it might have brought me to my knees, otherwise.

"That sounds lovely," I said softly.

"I've grown attached to the snakes, but sometimes I miss being able to plait my hair."

"Plait mine, then." Hells, the words flew from my lips before I could stop them.

"Really?" Her snakes' eyes wandered over my unbound waves and then back to my face.

It was too late for me to take it back. "Why not?"

Because I could barely keep hold of my senses as it was, that was why. I did not need her closer, her fingers tangled in my hair...

She smiled and all of my reservations fled.

"Turn around!" she said excitedly.

I did as she told me, thankful to not be facing her when my cheeks grew red. Her fingers slid into my hair and her nails raked lightly against my scalp, causing a shiver to make its way down my spine.

Long minutes passed in silence as she slowly worked my hair into a single braid.

"Does it always take so long?"

"I am a touch out of practice," she said.

"Perhaps next time it will be easier for you." Next time? What the Hells was I saying?

"You have lovely hair," she said after a slight pause.

I laughed softly. "I find it a bother more often than not."

"I love it. My hair was long like this once."

Well, that decided it. I would never be able to cut the length off again.

I turned to her abruptly, and thought I caught a flash of gold as she shut her eyes quickly. "If you were able to return to what you were before, would you?"

She sat quietly, obviously pondering my question. Her fingers thoughtlessly brushed against the braid she made.

"No," she said at last. "No, I'd rather not, I think."

I turned fully to face her. "Why is that?"

She leaned in a little closer and placed her hand atop mine. "If I were to return to the human I was before, my life would be quite short. It would not be long before you were alone, once more. How could I ever make such a decision?"

My eyes dropped to her mouth as she spoke. Her lips were so close to mine. I merely had to lean in and they would touch. I caught myself wondering what it would feel like– what she might taste like.

I turned from her, settling my attention on the far well. "Yes, well, I've done alright up until now."

A loud knock on the door made us both jolt where we sat. Her head turned to the door then back to me.

"Were you expecting company?" I asked.

She shook her head. "No. There is no one else here I know."

She stood and hurried to the door, cracking it open.

"Hello?"

"Evening, Gorgon," said a familiar voice– one that had plagued me for years. "I'm here for the Witch."

Medusa opened the door and stepped aside, and in sauntered Hermes.

16.

Star

He wore ivory robes and winged sandals– and a crooked smile that sang of mischief. He stepped into Medusa's home with a carefree air about him, but his attire was far more official than I had seen in a long time.

"Do you not have more important matters than spoiling my evening?" I said, marching toward them.

His smile widened and he gave a quick wink. "What on earth could be more important than this?"

I opened my mouth to fire a retort, but Medusa spoke first. "Would you care for some tea?"

She probably missed the way his eyes drug across her body, or his lips curling into a slight snarl, but I did not. If he did not watch himself, I would force my way into Tartarus– with him in tow.

"There's no need," I said, cutting him off as he was about to answer. "He is going to tell me what he needs to say, and then he'll be on his way."

Her face fell and she nodded. "Very well. I can give the two of you a moment."

"Thank you," Hermes said with a tone that implied it pained him to say it.

She turned to leave and I caught her hand. Her snakes swiveled to look at me.

"You can stay. Anything he has to say to me can be said in front of you."

"Are you sure about that?" he asked.

I turned to him and he stared at me– challenging me.

"Quite," I said with gritted teeth.

He shrugged. "Suit yourself. Hades has orders for you."

"Orders?" I echoed. "I do not take orders."

Medusa's fingers tightened around mine, reminding me I had not let go of her hand. The gentle squeeze soothed my frustration slightly.

Hermes smiled, glancing around Medusa's home. "Oh, I think you will today."

"And why is that?"

He stepped around me and then backed against the counter, keeping his eyes locked with mine. "This could change the course of the future. The Underworld, the mortal lands… maybe even Olympus."

I glared at him. He was up to something. There was far too much excitement in his eyes for him to just be following orders. I glanced at Medusa. Her expression was as wary as I felt– and she did not even know Hermes the way I did.

"What does Hades want her to do?" she asked.

I looked at him again. My stomach was in knots as I waited for him to reply. Hades had always avoided confrontation. What sort of future defining thing could he possibly be planning?

"He wants you to move into the mortal lands."

"The mortal lands? Why?" I failed to see how that would have such a large scale impact on the world.

Hermes rolled his eyes, as if the answer to my question was obvious. "For the Goddess of Spring. He believes Demeter plans to hide her there, if she hasn't already."

I scoffed. I had assumed he had given up on the prophecy long ago. "Demeter hates Hades. There is no way she would risk having a child after The Fates foretold her future. Even if she did, she would never let her out of her sight."

He shrugged. "Hades seems to disagree."

"That is ridiculous. I'll not move my entire life to the mortal lands so Hades can *possibly* find a wife. If he wants her so badly, let him find her himself."

"Shall I tell him that is your answer?"

"Yes!" I snapped. "I am not some underling or hound, here to do his bidding. Tell the bastard to send his harlot Nymph."

Hermes cackled before being swallowed by a bright light and vanishing.

Silence followed his departure. Not the peaceful kind I once reveled in– but one of dread and unease. Something big was coming. It carried through the air like a distant war cry, then the whispers found me again. Their words were clear this time, even in the ancient tongue I had not heard in several hundred years, I knew what they said.

"She's coming."

"Life. Death. Light and darkness."

"The beginning and the end."

"Persephone."

I shuddered. Why would she come after so many years? There was no way it was possible. The Fates had failed their prophecy.

"The Goddess of Spring?" Medusa mused quietly.

I turned to look at her, my hand still clutching hers. "He's wrong. There is no Goddess of Spring, and there never will be."

"But if there's a chance–"

"If there is a chance, she deserves better than this hellscape and the pompous ass who runs it."

Medusa flinched, but she said nothing.

"She would wither here amongst the iron," I continued. "This is no place for such a Goddess."

And I had no intention of bringing her to him, even if I did find her one day.

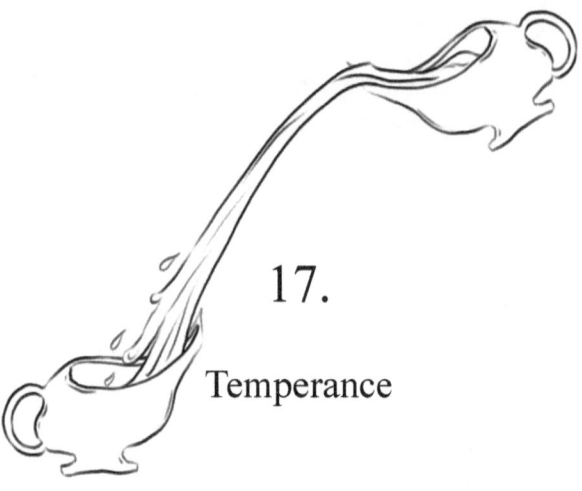

17.

Temperance

I expected Hades to be more insistent on the matter; for him to send Hermes repeatedly or show up at my home demanding me to do as he said.

But weeks came and went with no sign of him.

My days were spent with Medusa; the two of us drying herbs and embroidering. My nights were spent tossing and turning. Sleep evaded me as thoughts of the future and whispers from The Fates haunted every moment of peace I might have had.

"Hades has been just and fair," Medusa said one morning as we walked from her home to mine. "Perhaps you should help him– it may put your mind at ease."

"I cannot in good faith be the reason she is brought here. *Spring.* That will be her domain. This place will be too desolate for her."

"She is supposed to bring change, no?"

I glanced at Medusa as we walked. Her face was straight ahead, but her snakes stared back at me. "Hades was also supposed to bring change to this place."

And I had witnessed first hand how well that had gone.

A small smile spread across her face. "You always have ill-turned words to say about him, but he has done more for me than most."

I rolled my eyes and shook my head. "Wait until you've known him as long as I have."

She slid her arm into mine and leaned against me, igniting a fire across my cheeks. "Is there anyone you *do* like?"

"I am not that unpleasant," I said, narrowing my eyes at her.

She laughed, bright and carefree. Her joy was contagious and I could not keep the corners of my lips from turning up into a grin.

"You are not unpleasant at all. I believe you pretend to be far more irritable than you really are."

I barked a laugh. "I assure you– that much is not fake."

The conversation between us died after that, but it was a comfortable stillness that hung in the air. As soon as the roof of the hut came into view, however, I was stricken with nausea. It had been longer than I could recall since I had done any sort of grand gesture for anyone. And though the details were fuzzy, I was sure it had not made me so nervous.

As I reached for the door handle, I decided if she was unsatisfied I would take Hades up on his request and I would disappear into the mortal realm for the rest of my days.

I pushed the door open and stepped aside. Medusa walked up to the doorway, her snakes eyeing me suspiciously, and then she gasped. Her eyes flew open, and I caught a flash of gold before I could squeeze my own eyes shut.

"Hecate…" Her voice trailed off.

Her steps were soft on the hardwood floor as she walked further into the room. My eyes were closed, but I was sure everything was exactly as I left it. Hours upon hours were spent gathering flowers from the world above. If anyone had asked me how long it had taken, I might have lied.

They were bunched in bouquets on every surface I could manage, and in the end I had resorted to putting them on the floor.

"It's nothing big. I just thought you might like a piece of the upperworld. They will not last long, of course, but–"

I was cut off by a sudden embrace. Her arms wrapped around my neck and she buried her face in my shoulder.

"Thank you," she said. "You have no idea how much this means to me."

Slowly, I opened my eyes and put my arms around her.

I could not remember the last time I had hugged someone. Her warmth seeped through my clothes– through my skin and bones– down into my soul, where the oily residue of Chaos slumbered. It stirred the echo of darkness awake, like she called to it somehow.

Or perhaps it views her as its prey, I thought as the power crept through me silently.

I was snapped from my mind, back into the moment, by her touch abruptly drifting. Her fingers slid under my hair, gliding along my bare neck, and I froze. Surely she felt the fire she kindled as it spread across my body.

She lifted her head and faced me, her eyes shut tightly. I did not bother looking at the snakes, I knew already they were looking at me. My attention was locked on Medusa's face, which was mere inches from my own. Her hand was still lightly around my neck, the other resting on my shoulder. Her scent encased me.

It was intoxicating.

My eyes dipped to her lips. Hells, what was I doing? I could not think straight with her so close to me. Somewhere, in the back of my mind, I knew I needed to let her go– to back away– but the thought was lost to the heat growing low in my stomach and my heart pounding in my ears.

Instead of heeding my own warning, my hand wandered to her hip and my fingers dug into her. Her lips parted and she let out a soft gasp. It was nearly enough to make me release her except…

Her hands held me closer, pulling me flush against her.

My face grew hotter. Her lips were so close to mine, her breath feathered across my face.

"Medusa," I whispered, but the words that were supposed to come after died on my tongue before I could say them.

What was I trying to say? What was it that I wanted?

Her fingers traced their way from my neck to my jaw, her touch so gentle the hair on my arms raised. Then they drifted to my lips. I reached up, taking her wrist, and I pressed a kiss into her fingers.

Even as I did it, guilt stirred around and melded with the heat pooling between my thighs,

What I was doing was wrong. I should have stopped–
But I did not.

I kissed her wrist next, then just a little further up her arm. Her skin was soft, her smell earthy and rich.

She reached out and tucked a wave of hair behind my ear. I lost my breath; never had anyone made me lose myself so entirely. Her eyes cracked open, not quite enough for me to see them, but enough to tell she was staring at my lips.

Hells, I wanted her to look at me. I wanted to really see her. I wondered if it would truly turn me to stone, or if the old magic that coursed through my veins would keep me safe.

At that moment, I thought it might be worth the risk.

My hands moved on their own, and I cupped her face. She would hate me forever if I took advantage of her. She would never want to see me again.

There was a tug and tightness in my chest, urging me to press my mouth to hers. All I had to do was lean in.

My heart raced, my face was on fire.

What was I doing?

I moved to kiss her, the risks be damned, but just before our lips met, there was a loud banging on my door.

The sudden sound made me recoil. The tug at my chest might as well have been severed, but the heat in my cheeks lingered like a forgotten fire pit whose flames struggled to stay alive.

Loud bangs continued as I slipped past her to answer whoever so desperately needed me.

I swung my door open, thinking solely of how close I had been to ruining the only friendship I had, but the thought fell into an all devouring abyss as a blood soaked God collapsed into my arms, weeping.

18.

Three of Swords

The next several minutes were a whirlwind.

Time somehow stopped and also sped up all around me. Medusa rushed to grab wet linens to clean him up, and threw a pot of water over the small stove fire to steep tea. She urged the dogs into my bed chamber and closed the door.

I was stuck at my place by the entrance of my home, nearly as covered in blood as he was. It was impossible to decipher what happened between his uncontrollable sobbing.

"Slow down, Hypnos! Breathe."

I grabbed his face in my hands and coached him through three long breaths. He choked several more gulps of air, wiping his blood stained hands across his eyes. When he finally settled, I spoke again.

"What the Hells happened?"

His bottom lip trembled. "Cassandra."

My heart sank. His human partner. I was unsure how long the two had been involved– I did not socialize with him in a way to know his private life, but it had spread like a raging wildfire amongst the Gods. I had heard of it from Aphrodite. She lived for gossip.

Gossip.

Viewing it in such a way while looking at him in the state he was in… it put a sour taste in my mouth.

"What happened to her?" It was an insensitive question, but given the circumstances, it seemed warranted.

His face fell. "Nyx. Nyx killed her."

The answer hit me forcefully. His own mother. My eyes flicked across his fair skin, splattered with deep red blood, and my back went rigid. Whatever she had done, it must have been gruesome.

I brushed his long, dark hair from his face. It was also soaked in his lover's blood. "Oh, darling, I am so sorry."

"I-I tried to convince Thanatos not to take her. I begged him." More tears streamed down his cheeks.

I squeezed his hand in mine. "You know your brother could not have brought her back. Even if he did not bring her here, she would still be gone."

"I know." His voice was strangled. "'Mortals are weak; their lives are fleeting.' That is what Nyx said to me."

I cringed. Of course her words were true, but she had a cruel streak that everyone seemed to avoid discussing– and a particular distaste for mortals.

"Come," Medusa said, taking his arm and gently leading him into the kitchen. "Let us get you cleaned up and get something warm in your belly."

He let her guide him to the table and sat quietly while she cleaned him. I poured his tea and set the cup in front of him. It would not erase his troubles, but it would relax his body.

Once he was mostly clean, and drank half of his tea, he spoke again, his voice as hollow as his heart must have been. "Thanatos said he would make sure she drank from Lethe. I don't want her to remember the torment she suffered at the hands of Nyx."

It was then, in that moment, I finally understood why Lethe existed; why it was so instrumental to the Underworld and the souls that moved on. Mortal minds could not hold onto such anguish forever.

My eyes flicked to Medusa. Her face was soft, but her hands were clasped so tightly in her lap, her knuckles were white.

Would she have been better off if I had encouraged her to partake in the gift of the river?

Her snakes raised their heads to look at me, and as if she could read my mind, she subtly shook her head.

I turned my attention back to Hypnos, I could fret over my shortcomings with Medusa later. "I'm sure Lethe will bring her peace, dear. Know there was nothing you could have done–"

"I could have cut ties with her the first time Nyx tried to convince me," he interrupted.

I paused. In truth, I had no idea what to say. He was right. Had he ended things with the human, she would not have met such an end. I was not good at comforting people, nor was I a skilled liar. There was nothing more I could do for him.

"You loved her– Cassandra." We both turned to look at Medusa. A single tear slid down her cheek. "Not everyone is so fortunate to have been truly loved. I'd wager, if you were able to ask her, she'd tell you it was worth it."

His chin trembled. "We did not have long enough together. We should have... We should have had more time."

She reached across the table and took his hand. "I watched my grandmother grieve over the loss of my grandfather. They grew up together– spent every day loving each other. He passed when he was very old, yet, my grandmother wept those same words.

"'We should have had more time.' 'It wasn't enough.' The things you are feeling are normal. There would never have been enough time."

Hypnos buried his face in his arms and cried. It was the sound of a shattered heart; of someone who was no longer whole. I had never witnessed love like that before, but I told myself then and there if I found it, I would never let it go.

I looked across the table at Medusa, who was petting Hypnos' head, consoling him.

The tightness in my chest returned. I sat quietly, taking slow, shallow breaths as I watched her calm him once more. She was beautiful, and kind; her heart beat to soothe those who were hurting.

And I had nearly destroyed my friendship with her because of my selfishness.

I would do better for her, moving forward.

I would *be* better.

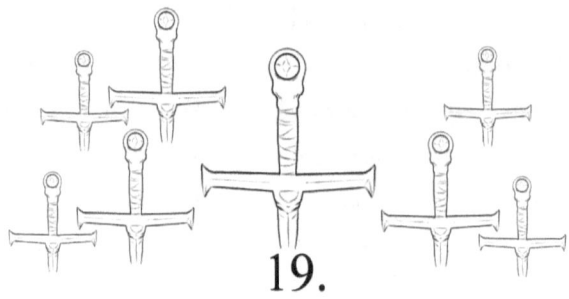

19.

Eight of Swords

Several days came and went– and Medusa did not visit me. Although time was hard to tell in the Underworld; the sky stayed a dusted gray, no matter what time it was– no sun or moon to mark the hour.

My home had been quiet, my dogs restless.

I had ruined things with her, afterall. She had no doubt decided to steer clear of me, and I could not blame her for it.

I'd never admit I spent those days mostly curled up in bed, not even bothering to change from my nightclothes. Guilt and shame and sadness mingled together to envelope me in one grand pity party.

But not on this particular day.

No, on this day I forced myself out of bed. I dressed myself, and braided my hair back in one single plait, like Medusa had done for me before.

And I walked.

Gray sky above me, and black iron under my feet, I made my way to a tall peak that jutted up from the ground. I tried not to think as I walked. Not about why I could not bring myself to use my power, or the fact I had not seen Medusa in days. My entire reason for going out was to do something selfless. To do something for someone else.

I craned my head up toward the cove of the spire. There would be no getting around using my magic, if I was going to go up and see him. I sighed and raised my hands, but I paused.

Perhaps I should have asked before I showed up unannounced. He might not even want to see me at all. My hands fell to my sides as I stared up, feeling hollowed and empty.

"Are you alright?"

I whirled around and my gaze fell on Hypnos. He was standing there, dark circles under his eyes, and a small satchel at his hip.

I blinked at him. Once. Twice.

"I–" I paused again.

My stomach knotted and twisted inside me as I searched for anything to say. I was not good with words, and certainly I was not a good friend. Why I ever thought it was a good idea to try and be there for him was beyond me.

"I came to check on you," I continued.

His brows twitched and he glanced from me to the river, and back again. "That is very kind of you."

Silence rang in my ears as we looked at each other.

"I should go," I said.

He turned as I brushed past him and grabbed the sleeve of my dress gently. "Wait."

When I looked at him, his eyes welled with tears. "You can stay," he whispered. "I think I might like the company."

It was no wonder he had found love in the mortal realm. He was soft, gentle natured, unlike the other Gods.

I nodded slowly. "I brought tea, if you would like."

He smiled, though it was slight and forced. He looked as uncomfortable as I felt. "That sounds lovely."

He turned his palm up, offering me his hand, and I took it. Dust and debris from the iron swirled around us as he whisked us into his small cove– his home. I tried not to inspect it as I walked further in and settled myself on a loose chunk of iron. He probably had as few visitors as I did, and I was sure he felt exposed having me there.

I pulled two small clay cups from my own bag, and set them down on the floor, pouring loose tea into them, and then water. When I held my hands over them to draw on my dark magic to heat the tea, I nearly became sick.

Medusa flinching flashed in my mind, and I attempted to brush it away. Still, the nausea lingered.

"How have you been since I last saw you?" I choked on the words as I forced my power to flow, igniting a small flame to heat our tea.

"I've been better."

My eyes flicked up to his tired face and I closed my eyes slowly. It was a stupid question– one I should not have bothered with.

"I'd imagine." I passed him a cup. "Have you looked for her?"

Another distasteful question.

"No. I–" he paused. "I cannot bring myself to do it. I don't want to risk upsetting her."

Slowly we fumbled our way through conversation. Regardless of the awkwardness, he started to relax. Hours passed us, and talking to each other became easier.

Finally, I stood, brushing my hands against the skirt of my dress. "Well, I should be going. I implore you to try and rest, Hypnos. Sleep, if you can."

He smiled up at me from his place on the floor of the small cave. "Thank you, Hecate, for spending this time with me."

I gave him a small nod. "Of course. If you need anything at all, let me know."

As my magic enveloped me to take me home, there was a shift in the air. Some sort of disturbance, like something, or someone, had tread somewhere they should not have.

Something was off.

It stirred my senses, putting me on edge in a way I had not been in a long while.

When I appeared outside of my home, I froze. I stood there for several long seconds, trying to find the source of my unease. Everything looked normal, but there was power in the air. It was soft, like it lingered from being used earlier. Then I caught a familiar smell.

I pushed the door open and stormed inside, rushing straight to the kitchen.

Hermes sat at my table, drinking a cup of tea he obviously helped himself to.

"*What* are you doing in my home?"

His eyes lifted to mine from over the lip of the cup. "Finally! I was starting to wonder if you would ever come back."

I looked down at the pack of dogs, all curled at his feet. "You are all useless," I muttered. My attention settled back on him, my eyes narrowing. "What do you want, Hermes?"

He set the cup down so abruptly it splashed tea onto the table. "Hades is requesting you at his manor. He said it's urgent."

He did not even bother to glance at his mess, let alone clean it up.

"Tell Hades I have no interest in arguing with him about Demeter's daughter again."

He shoved himself to his feet, nearly knocking the chair over onto the floor. "I'm afraid I cannot bring him two refusals in a row, Witch. I'm going to need you to pay him a visit."

"I–"

"*You*," Hermes snarled, losing his composure, "can deal with his little tantrum on your own. I've been at the brunt end of it once already, and I do not particularly care to do it again."

Silence fell between us as Hermes took a deep breath, trying to regain control over himself.

I sighed. "You are quite insufferable, did you know that?"

He flashed me a fake smile. "I was thinking the same of you."

I put my palms flat on the table and leaned over it, toward him. "Get out of my house."

"Fine. But if you leave him waiting, just know I'll come right back here and drag you to him if I must."

"Oh, I am sure you will."

He stepped up to brush past me and stopped, leaning in. "You are idle while the future hangs in the balance, Witch. The rest of us are being proactive. You might give it a try."

And in a flash of light– he was gone.

I looked down at Hecuba and her ears perked up. "You could not have at least bitten him?"

Her tail thumped against the floor and amusement danced in her eyes. With annoyance for both Hermes and Hades, I lifted my palm and called on my magic. The slick residue of Chaos tried to slip into it and I closed my eyes to focus. It was becoming harder and harder to separate the feel of my power and the feel of what Chaos left with me.

Then a plume of purple smoke rippled around me and swallowed me.

***

I appeared outside of Hades' gloomy manor. At first, everything was still and quiet. There was not much below to cause noise, especially outside of The Furies' territories. All the Underworld had to give was iron and cursed rivers, and neither of those things had much to say.

But then– then I heard raised voices from inside the manor. I leaned against the door and strained my ears. I couldn't quite make out what was being said, but the shrill tone to the woman's voice told me it was Minthe. The other voice was not Hades, and that was all I needed, to know I could still enter.

Interrupting anyone else did not bother me in the slightest. Though, if I was being quite honest, I might have enjoyed seeing an argument between him and Minthe.

When I pushed the door open and stepped into the throne room the voices fell silent. It was Minthe and Thanatos, the twin brother of Hypnos and close council of Hades. I should have guessed.

"What?" Minthe snapped at me.

I arched a brow and my eyes slid to Thanatos. His arms were crossed and he was wearing a deep frown.

"She's rather perturbed today, it seems," he sneered.

She whirled at him, her blue eyes wild, and pointed her finger in his face. "I am not *perturbed*– I am outraged!"

I rolled my eyes and made to stalk past them. "It feels as though this has nothing to do with me, so if you'll excuse me."

Minthe stormed up beside me. "It has *everything* to do with you!"

I halted and looked at her. "What the Hells have I done to you?"

"Hades is sending you out to look for Demeter's precious daughter and–"

"Enough, Nymph." I waved her off. "I have no intention of bringing Demeter's daughter here, so take your *'outrage'* elsewhere."

I did not give her time to respond before I walked off, leaving her and Thanatos alone in the throne room.

The doors to the dining hall were closed, as they always were. I placed my hands on them to push them open and paused. I remembered the first time Hades invited me to his home. He was far younger then, filled with hope and excitement, despite his short draw on realms.

'Close the door behind you,' he had said. *'It leaves a draft if it's left open.'*

A draft. It seemed silly to me at the time, there was no wind in the lands below to cause such a thing. Yet, after spending so long in the land of iron, I could feel it. A slight draft, a whisper of a wind hanging in the air. I had resorted to keeping all of my doors closed, as well.

I shook off the memory and pushed the heavy doors open, pulling them closed behind me.

There he was– sitting at the head of his table that was far too long for the small circle of people that regularly visited his home. Empty plates and glasses were positioned at each of the seats, as if he expected to host a party at a moment's notice.

"Good evening, Witch."

There that blasted word was again.

I walked over and took a seat at the table, glaring at Hades. His face was... tired. I had never seen him look so disheveled.

"You summoned me?

"You refused my request for your help in finding Demeter's daughter."

"It sounded more like a demand. I believe Hermes referred to it as an '*order*'."

Seconds ticked by as we stared at each other in silence.

"I cannot leave the Underworld long enough to make any real progress looking for her, myself."

"And why does it have to be me?" I pushed. "Send someone else."

"I thought maybe you had some sort of," he paused, "spell that would help."

I barked a laugh. "If only it were so simple. I would need a lock of hair, or some blood, for a spell like that."

His brows furrowed. "You could–"

"Spend the rest of my life searching? Check every corner of the earth? Go to Demeter and beg her?"

His lip curled into a snarl.

I knew I was pushing him a bit too far, but I was still raw from all that had transpired between me and Medusa. Perhaps this would teach him not to send Hermes to my home unannounced.

"The Fates said–"

"I don't care what The Fates said!" I snapped.

He flinched and his eyes dipped to the dark magic building around me. "You seem more irritable than normal," he said.

"I am."

The Fates had made many prophecies over my lifetime, all of which had come true. Except the one regarding Demeter's daughter. That was the last one they ever made. Probably because they had been wrong.

"What can I do to convince you?" His voice was softer; full of desperation.

"There is nothing you could offer me to get me to agree, Hades. I will not be a part of this."

He sighed and leaned back in his seat. "Cerberus is doing well. He's getting quite big."

The sudden change in subject caught me off guard, and my body relaxed. "Hopefully he is causing you less trouble than he did for me."

He chuckled, and for a moment I saw a hint of the God I knew before. "He's chewed a few pieces of furniture, but he's smart and he's learning."

"That's good."

How long had it been since the two of us had such a mundane conversation? There was a time, long ago, when the two of us were fairly pleasant with one another. I couldn't even remember when that had changed.

His eyes flicked to mine and he pushed himself up from the table. "I will continue to ask you, Hecate. Even if I must get on my knees and beg."

He brushed past me, making his way to the stairs.

"Next time, give me a heads up. I'll make something for us to eat while we argue."

"I like apple pie," he said over his shoulder.

Then he sauntered off, up the stairs and into his bedchamber, leaving me alone at his table.

Silence fell over the room. It was thick, nearly strangling me, as I mulled over the events that had taken place recently. Medusa, Hades' sudden obsession with finding the Goddess of Spring, the cruelty of Nyx and heartbreak of Hypnos, my fight with Athena. The strange whispers from the Fates…

It was all too much for me. It crushed in on me, making it hard to breathe. I wanted nothing more than just a sliver of peace, again. A moment of happiness.

That all seemed rather far away– sitting just outside of my reach. I wasn't even sure I had ever had it to begin with.

I pulled at my magic again, and spirited myself away from the dreary castle of Hades, back to my home.

Hecuba stood up and stretched, then walked over to me. I stared down into her dark eyes and her tail wagged softly.

"All is well," she might have said. *"Do not fret over things beyond your control."*

"Would that I could, dear one. Would that I could."

There was a soft knock at my door, and my head snapped up.

Who in the name of the Hells needs me now? I thought.

I stood up, and the pack of dogs rushed to follow me. I swung the door open, fully intending to shoo whoever it was away. There had been quite enough for me to deal with, without something new being added to the mix.

But my heart sputtered when my eyes fell on her, and my chest grew so tight I thought I might burst. Heat rose to my cheeks, and my mind cleared of all of the turmoil that haunted it just seconds before.

"Medusa?" I breathed.

She stepped into my home, and I retreated to give her space. Her face was tense, her brows knitted together. I expected her to lash out at me– to scold me for the way I had behaved days prior. To tell me she did not want me to ever touch her like that again.

But what actually came out of her mouth caused the world to shatter around me. I thought I must have heard her wrong, or been hallucinating all together.

There was no way she said what I thought she did.

Oh, but she had indeed said what I thought she did.

"I want you to remove my eyes."

And she meant it.

20.

The Tower

"I want you to remove my eyes."

I was not sure what happened in the days I had not seen her, but somehow she had managed to lose her mind. No sane person would ask someone to do that.

"Medusa, you cannot be serious."

She slipped past me, making her way into the kitchen. I followed along behind her, the dogs trailing after me.

"I am," she said, rummaging through drawers and cabinets. "You must have something here that could help ease the pain once it is done."

I reached out and took her arm, and she whirled to face me. "Medusa, this is insanity. You don't mean–"

"I do mean it!" she snapped.

I dropped her arm and took a step back.

"I'm tired of this," she continued. "I live every single second of my life in fear I will accidentally look at you. I've almost done it several times already– I know you're aware of it."

My shoulders drooped. "Yes, well... You haven't."

"But I could." Her voice cracked with fear and desperation. The snakes atop her head bobbed and weaved, like the pain she felt also plagued them.

My eyes dropped to the floor, and then flicked back up to her face. My heart strained– torn on whether I should do what she wanted or refuse her.

"It will be easier on both of us if you let me use my power." As the words left my lips, nausea settled in my stomach.

Fuck... Could I really watch her writhe and scream as I took her eyes?

"No," she said sternly. "No power."

The fierceness in her expression was nearly enough to turn me to stone without her cursed stare. If I hadn't known all she'd been through, I might have thought her naive, or ignorant to the pain she would be in if I took a knife to her face.

But that was not the case, at all.

She knew exactly what she was asking of me, and how badly it would hurt. Her shoulders were squared, her body tense. The amount of determination she was showing might have frightened anyone else, but not me. Somehow the way she steeled herself in the face of what she was asking only made my heart grow fonder for her.

She was much stronger than I had given her credit for.

I stepped forward and placed my hand against her cheek. "I will not insult you by telling you how awful this will be, or by telling you what a terrible idea I believe this is."

She reached up and brushed her fingers against mine. "Thank you."

For a moment, something solidified between us. I was no God, no Titan or Witch, and she was no Gorgon. We were just... two souls whose fate strings had intertwined somewhere along the way.

Her hand dropped from mine, and in its absence I became chilled. Gooseflesh raised along my arms, and the air around us became heavy, as if the very essence of the Underworld knew what was about to take place.

I ushered the dogs and Galinthias into the bedroom, but Hecuba lingered behind.

"Go," I said, softly. "You will not want to witness this."

Her ears laid against her head and she let out a high pitched whine. I knelt beside her and ran my fingers through her thick coat. It was easy, sometimes, to think of her as a dog. But really, was she any more a dog than Medusa was a beast?

"Fine. You may stay. Just..." *Don't think of me differently*, I wanted to say. *Don't hate me for what I am about to do.*

She leaned forward and rested her head on my shoulder, her tail thumping slowly against the floor. A sign of understanding and solidarity. She had seen me do wonderful and terrible things, but nothing so gruesome as this. Yet, still, she stood beside me and my decisions.

I gave her one final scratch behind the ear and then stood, turning to Medusa. Her shoulders were still squared, her back straight, but her arms were wrapped tightly around herself. I had to trust she would tell me if she changed her mind– I would not treat her like a child who could not decide things for herself.

"Come," I said. "We need to prepare you for what is about to happen."

She followed me over to a small table, one covered in bottled herbs and half burnt candles. I took a vial of poppy seeds, poured them into a mortar, and then ground them down with a pestle. It took everything in me not to chant over my work, to imbue it with magic that would make it more potent.

I did not want her to feel any pain.

But I would respect her wishes. I would do things the mortal way, regardless of how it made me feel. Because this was not about me, it was about her– how she felt, and the power this was giving her back as it took a piece of what Athena had done to her.

I lit a small bundle of herbs and smoked the bowl, cleansing the seeds she was about to ingest.

Silence hung between us, and the space grew solemn. I waved the burning herbs over a sharpened knife, the one I was about to use to cut Medusa's eyes from her head.

Nausea rolled through me, and I swallowed. Never had I been more nervous than I was at that moment. It would haunt me for the rest of my days. It would spoil my sleep and my appetite, lingering in my mind during my waking hours.

My soul hovered somewhere over my body as I stirred the poppy seeds into a glass of moon water, and watched as she downed it all in one gulp.

"Should I sit at the table?" she asked.

I wanted to laugh, but it would have come out garbled and terrified. "I'd think you might want to lay on the floor."

She paused, then moved to lie down. Her body was tense, and her movements stiff. She must have been as nervous as I was.

Good. It meant she hadn't lost her mind, after all.

Numbness crept up my arm as I reached for the dagger I had cleansed moments before. It was much heavier in my hand than it had been in the past, weighed down by the task it was being made to perform.

I leaned over Medusa, and her throat bobbed. "This will be your last chance, Dear One. Once the blade meets your flesh, there will be no turning back."

She reached up and grabbed the collar of my dress in her fist, pulling me close. All of her fear melted away and a ferociousness I had not seen before, replaced it. "I don't care how much I scream or beg you, don't stop."

Time halted around us as I stared at her. My heart swelled and tears stung my eyes. How had she come to mean so much to me? How did she go from a wailing Gorgon that was ruining my life to–

I leaned down and pressed my lips to her forehead. "I am so sorry."

The next moment, my body was not my own. Once more, I was hovering over us, watching from above as I held Medusa down and carved out her eyes. It was no easy task, fighting her instincts to stop me, while I kept my eyes closed tightly.

Her screams shattered the Underworld in a way that later made me wonder if it would ever be the same, or if we had tainted it. Sullied its essence forever with our brutality.

And while her flesh was sliced open by my hand, I felt that familiar tug at my chest, and the whispers of The Fates. I could not decipher what they said, though. They were drowned out by Medusa's screaming.

21.

Justice

Blood was caked and dried along my clothes and my skin, causing every move I made to be tight and stiff. It was so uncomfortable I had resorted to sitting as still as I could.

I stared at the bloodied wall and floor, but I was not looking at it– not really. My mind drifted and stilled; had become silent.

It had been hours since I had maimed Medusa, and it had taken her almost as long to fall asleep.

Her screams echoed in my ear, startling me out of my trance, but when I snapped to, there was only quiet.

I brought my hand up, and lightly brushed my fingers along the carnage that was dried on my cheek. Before any real thought had time to form, I pushed myself up from the table and busied myself with cleaning and scrubbing all of the evidence away. I wanted every speck gone before she woke.

It would have been easy to cast a spell to rid the room of what I had done; to snap my fingers and it be gone. But Medusa's stern request before we started replayed in my head.

No power.

My arms trembled, my muscles weak and sore, as I desperately scrubbed the floor with a stiff bristled brush. I did not feel the tears coming until they streamed down my face.

A soft sob slipped from my lips and my vision blurred, tears contorting the blood into a smear of red across my eyes.

The Gods were cruel, the world was cruel, and I... I was cruel.

The brush fell from my shaking hand and clattered to the floor. I was wrapped in the darkness of my candlelit cabin, swaddled in the blackness of my soul and my magic. The essence of Chaos crept in, cradling me, and I wept unabashedly with my face buried in my hands.

A quiet whine cut through my cries and I lifted my face to meet Hecuba. Her ears were laid back and her brown eyes were full understanding. I glanced down at her paws.

She was standing in a puddle of blood that had been refreshed with the water I was using to try and clean it.

I found myself questioning everything I had ever done. Was it all a mistake?

My lips trembled. "I don't know what I am doing," I admitted to her. "I am lost."

She stepped closer and laid down next to me, resting her head in my lap, unbothered by the blood that was soaking into her dark fur.

"You are not lost," her eyes said. *"You are the one who guides the way."*

120

I reached out and tangled my fingers into her fur. "I am no guide. I am just blinding darkness."

She nudged me with her nose and tilted her head. *"No. You are like the moon– scattering the darkness of night."*

My shoulders shook and I collapsed into her, crying all of the tears I had tucked away for so long. Every wound I had believed to be healed and closed, ripped open and bled again.

She allowed me time to grieve and weep, laying underneath me patiently as I emptied myself. And when I sat up, cleansed from the tears I cried, I felt lighter– renewed.

She was right. I had made difficult decisions, made choices that would have broken others, and I made it out whole– leading the way for those that I kept near me. I lifted the torch high, casting away all of the shadows.

The terrible things I had done held purpose. I was feared once. I had stood tall and firm in what I believed.

But I had also been revered.

That Titan; that Goddess, the beast that I was… She was not gone. She had not left me stranded. In the depths of my soul, she lingered, waiting to be released. I had set her loose on Poseidon, and the King of the Gods sat there and watched.

Because I was not feared *once.*

I wiped the tears and blood from my face and grabbed the brush, scrubbing again at the carnage.

Titan. Witch. God.

Maiden, Mother, Crone.

I was The Trinity.

And I was *still* feared.

22.

Six of Cups

Medusa slept for days after what I did to her.

I wet her lips and cleaned her wounds, and at night I sat on a chair with my head resting on the bed beside her. Her sleep was fitful, and her tossing and turning left me exhausted each morning when I woke. The dogs rarely left her side, but I was not sure Hecuba or Galinthias ever did. I spiraled as she slept, wondering if I had done something wrong, if she would never wake at all.

The silence of the Underworld was thicker and more deafening than it was before, and it taunted my every waking moment while I waited for Medusa to regain consciousness.

On the third morning, she woke.

I lurched up and stared down at her as she stirred and pushed herself upright. Relief dropped heavy into my stomach and turned to nausea. She might fear me, after the pain I caused her– I was just another God who had harmed her.

"Good morning." Her voice was quiet and raspy.

A tear slid down my cheek. "Good morning, Medusa."

Quiet echoed between us, her snakes watching me intensely. "How long was I asleep?"

"Three days," I whispered. "I feared you would not wake."

She reached out and took my hand in hers, her fingers soft and cool against my skin. "I am sorry I worried you."

"Do not apologize. Your body and your mind needed the rest." My voice trailed off, my eyes sliding over the healing gouges across her face. *I am sorry*, I wanted to say. *Please forgive me for what I have done to you.*

As if she read my mind, she smiled softly, her brows pulling together. "You have nothing to apologize for, either, Hecate. I will never be able to thank you enough for what you've done for me."

I did not realize I was crying until she reached up and brushed a stream of tears from my face. Flashes of blood and the faint echo of her screams flashed through my mind. It was heinous, what I did, regardless of the fact it was her request. I inflicted pain and suffering on the kindest person to walk the earth, and I felt sure I would pay for it somehow.

I reached up and ran my thumb across the hand she placed on my cheek. "You must be starving, dear. Let me fetch you some food."

She smiled and nodded, but my eyes drifted to Hecuba as Medusa told me of her grumbling stomach. There was a twinkle in the dog's dark eyes, and it almost looked as if she was smiling with us.

"You have friends," she seemed to say. *"And family. You are not alone."*

Despite everything that happened, I believed her.

23.
The Lovers

Weeks flew by me quickly. Medusa healed, but the marks from what I had done would stay with her forever. It had not been clean or precise–crude scars marred her face. She did not seem to mind it at all.

I had freed myself from the guilt of it. She was happier, more carefree than she had been before.

I glanced over at her. She was sitting on the floor near me, her attention focused on her embroidery. I had given up on attempting it further, and instead, had nestled down on the floor with Hecuba in my lap, content to watch Medusa as she worked her needle quietly.

"You're staring," she said softly.

My heart skipped at the sound of her voice, and I averted my gaze. "Sorry."

"Do the scars bother you?"

My eyes flicked back to her. "Of course not."

Her snakes all raised their heads to look at me. "Do you find me hideous?"

I scoffed and waved at her playfully. "I could never."

Heat rose from my neck to my cheeks, though. Hideous? If anything it was quite the opposite. The scars did not take from her beauty in the slightest.

Hecuba rose abruptly and padded from the room without casting either of us a second glance. Medusa discarded her work on the floor and slid closer to me. I forced myself to stay turned from her, looking at the place Hecuba disappeared from. The last thing I wanted her to see was the flush in my face.

"Tell me," she said. "How do you find me, then?"

My eyes squeezed shut, and I bit my tongue before it could betray me. "I fail to see why that matters."

She laid her fingers on my jaw. My eyes snapped open, and she gently turned me toward her. "If it were anyone else, perhaps it wouldn't. But what *you* think matters to me."

Hells.

I searched her face. My gaze slid across her green skin and shimmer of scales, then dipped to her lips. They were full– curved perfectly.

And they looked soft.

I glanced down at the heavy rise and fall of her chest, then back up to her mouth. My breath hitched in my throat, my words fighting to be set free–

And they prevailed.

"I find you enchanting."

Her brows rose. "Enchanting?" she echoed.

My words continued to pour out, the dam was broken and there was nothing left holding them back. "You are the most beautiful woman I have ever laid eyes on. But more than that, you are resilient, and kind. You are thoughtful and gracious."

She leaned closer and my face grew even hotter.

"Go on," she whispered.

I inhaled a shaky breath. She was too close, her smell and her warmth filled me, blurring lines and muddling my senses. I lifted my hand and brushed my thumb along her cheek.

"I've hurt you enough already. I do not want to bring you more pain."

Disappointment flashed across her face, but it fell away quickly. She placed her hand atop mine when I tried to move it, and held it gently in place. My stomach flipped and I swallowed the large lump forming in my throat.

"I find you enchanting, as well." She leaned so close her lips feathered across my cheek, nearly wrecking every last drop of self control I had. "You have taken hold of my mind, Hecate, and my heart flutters when you are near. I have never met someone so gentle, yet so fierce."

My stomach dropped and my thighs clenched. "Medusa–"

Her fingers slid up my arm and her other hand reached out to cradle my neck. "I thought I'd never want anyone to touch me again. I thought I would live forever repulsed by the idea." She brushed her lips along the lobe of my ear and warmth pooled between my legs.

"Medusa," I said again, but it came out barely more than a breath.

"But you," she continued softly, "you have changed that. I lay awake at night thinking of you."

127

My hold on her face became more firm. "You have to stop." There was no fire to my words, though. I was begging her.

She pulled away. "Do you not feel the same?"

My hand slid from her face to her throat, then down to her collarbone that barely peeked from the neckline of her dress. "Of course I do, but–"

"Then kiss me."

My heart pounded in my chest. There was nothing I wanted more than to press my lips to hers. "I don't want to hurt you," I said.

"I am not so fragile, Hecate."

I took her hand in mine with the intention of moving it further from me, but I brought it to my mouth, instead. I pressed my lips to her wrist.

"I could kiss you," I said. "Every inch of you. But what if this goes wrong? What if you grow to hate me? Then what?"

She brushed my hair back. "What if you grow to hate me?"

I flinched. "That would never happen."

A smile tugged at her lips. "I feel the same about you."

I paused, staring at her. If it was what she wanted, and what I wanted… Why should I fight it? "If I make you uncomfortable, you must tell me immediately."

"I promise," she whispered.

I took her face in my hands, leaning in, and the touch caused my whole body to hum. I placed a kiss on her cheek softly. It sent a blast of heat through me and I became dizzy.

Her hand grazed my ribs and she kissed my cheek in return. It filled me with such a fire, I thought I might combust under her touch. I was nothing more than clay in her hands to shape as she wished.

After a shaky breath, I kissed the corner of her lips and she followed my lead.

"Kiss me," she breathed, her voice desperate.

I pressed my lips to hers, then pulled away. She leaned in and kissed me again, and that time I did not retreat. I gave in to the feel of her, kissing her harder. My tongue brushed against her bottom lip and she granted my request, her mouth parting for me. Her tongue slid across mine, and the kiss became more urgent– more hungry.

Her fingers dug into my ribs and she moaned softly. All of my reservations fled from me and I moved closer, guiding her back on the floor.

Once she was laying down completely, I pulled away, hovering over her, both of us breathing heavily. She reached up, her fingers trailed across the neckline of my dress, then traced their way down my breast, down my stomach to my thigh. She pulled the hem of my dress up, exposing skin, and her hand traveled up my leg.

The fear of what might happen dissipated. All of the concerns I had for bringing her more pain and suffering melted away. Her skin against mine blazed. How could any of this be bad? Surely The Fates had brought us together for a reason– and why not this?

I kissed her jaw, then her neck. "I have wanted you for a while," I said quietly.

She whimpered, her fingers finding my bare hip, and she ground me down against her. "Then take me."

I would have done anything she asked of me; I would have toppled kingdoms, burned down any realm that displeased her. The world would have crumbled at her feet, if she would have wished it.

My hand groped her breast greedily, and she sucked air in through her teeth. Her lips found mine again, and everything around me vanished into darkness.

There was no cabin, no Underworld, no Chaos. There were no Fates or omens.

Just the two of us, fumbling to remove our clothes, our bodies pressed tightly against each other. Heat and skin and sweat. Soft moans and cries as we gave into the feelings we had both been trying to ignore.

I had met both humans and Gods who had changed me over the years; had met those who taught me both hard and gentle lessons.

But never had anyone crawled so deep into who I was their soul melded with mine.

Until then.

Until Medusa.

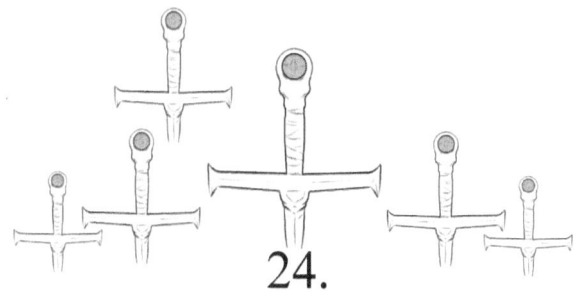

24.

Six of Swords

"Oh, please can I come with you this time?"

I glanced up at Medusa as she spoke. She was sitting across the table from me, Galinthias curled in her lap, sleeping– as usual. Her lips were pursed and her brows furrowed.

My eyes dipped to the steaming teacup in my hands, and I sighed. "That feels like a very unwise decision."

She lifted Galinthias and hugged her against her chest. The little creature dangled in her arms, her mind tucked into such a deep sleep she did not even stir at the act.

"Certainly there is somewhere secluded we could go?" she begged.

I brought the cup to my lips and blew gently before taking a sip. She was not wrong. My usual gathering place was well off the beaten path, and the only time I had ever encountered anyone, it was other Gods who had come specifically to look for me.

Yet, I could not shake the feeling something would go terribly wrong. It fell over me like a wet blanket, heavy and smothering.

"I don't know," I said, shaking my head slowly.

She laid Galinthias down on the table, rousing her from her nap. The little beast yawned and stretched her long body, and then curled back down and closed her eyes again.

Medusa pushed herself up from the table and carefully stepped over the heap of dogs on the floor, then knelt at my feet. Her hands grazed my knees, and I looked down at her.

"I'll be quiet," she said. "And at the first sign of anyone, we can leave."

She was pouting. That sort of thing had never worked on me before, but there I was– staring down at her with a sudden change of heart. She had me wrapped around her finger; my heart in her hands. How was I ever to tell her no?

A defeated sigh left my lips, and I set my cup on the table. "Fine," I said, then placed a kiss on her brow. "But we go quietly, we gather the herbs I need, and then we leave. We are not going to dally."

She nodded excitedly. "Yes, of course!"

Hells below and Heavens above. How long would it be before she realized she could have whatever she wanted from me?

***

"I hadn't a clue there were caves like this here," she whispered.

Despite her hushed voice, her words echoed through the deep cavern, bouncing off of the iron walls and reverberating around us. Water dripped from the ceiling and fell into stagnant puddles, rippling the surface.

"There are many caves in the Underworld, some safe to access, and others... Not so much." Some housed gruesome monsters who had sought refuge in the darkness of the caves after being hunted by Hades when he took hold of the Underworld. One especially dark, and especially deep cave, was home to The Fates.

At least that was what I had been told.

I saw no point in divulging that information to her while we were steadily venturing further into the darkness, though. There was no sense in scaring her more than she already was. She looked as though she was holding onto the contents of her stomach by a thread.

"And this one leads to the mortal realm?" she asked.

My fingers tightened around the torch in my hand and I lifted it higher over my head. We were coming to the crossroads.

"Yes," I said softly. "It would be much quicker and easier to get there the way I typically do, but this way works. Not many others know this path, and fewer still can navigate it. If it were not such a complicated labyrinth of passages, Hades might have closed it off long ago."

She stumbled over loose iron fragments on the cave floor and leaned into me for support, her arm wrapped tightly around mine.

"I could not imagine many would want to enter this place, even if they knew of it. It is quite unsettling," she said.

My eyes flicked to her face. Soft light danced across the curve of her cheekbone, shadows finding a home in her scales. "You'd be surprised what mortals would do to see their deceased loved ones again."

"I looked for my mother when I came here," she said, her voice barely audible.

It hadn't even occurred to me her own loved ones would be in the land of the dead. "Did you find her?"

She paused. The steady dripping of the cave water was all that kept it from being eerily silent, that and the crunch of our boots on the iron ground.

"I did, but she did not remember me. It seemed she drank from Lethe when she arrived."

My heart sank, but I did not have time to linger on the sadness that tried to creep around inside me, for the crossroads came into view. I raised the torch again and gave a quick glance down either path. It had been a long while since I had walked the caves to the upperworld, but the way forward would no doubt be burned in my mind forever.

"Come," I said, urging her down the right fork. "We're nearly there now."

We spent the rest of our time walking quietly. Indeed, it was not long before we met the first signs of the world above. The toe of my boot knocked into a loose pebble, kicking it into the wall, and dozens of wings flapped above us, small screeching shattering the quiet, as the creatures overhead abandoned their resting place and flew further down our path toward the exit.

Medusa's grip on me had tightened, her knuckles white. "Were those bats?"

I chuckled, leaning in and placed a kiss on her temple. "Yes. Just bats."

"Does that mean we are no longer in the Underworld?" Excitement brimmed her voice.

"That is exactly what that means. Welcome to the human realm, dear."

25.

Queen of Pentacles

Vibrant pinks and blues melted into a deep purple across the evening sky. The sun hung low, slowly giving way to nightfall. Heat from the day lingered, offering to us a small glimpse of the power the summer sun had over the mortal realm.

My attention to all of those things was fleeting, though, as my eyes fell on Medusa.

Her lips parted, her mouth falling slightly agape. Awe and wonder was plastered across her face, her hands pressed against her chest.

I said nothing as I allowed her to drink in the moment– to experience all the sights and smells I knew she had missed for so long. The mortal realm was beautiful, even I could not deny that. It was magical, in its own way. A quiet and subtle magic, one most Gods– or people, for that matter– might take for granted.

I had also taken it for granted.

Medusa took a slow step forward, her boots pressing against the grass in a way that made me wonder if she hated to disturb it at all. Her snakes' heads swiveled, their golden eyes wide.

I watched her turn and lift her head to the towering branches above us. If there was ever a person who did not take the surface world's beauty and magic for granted– it was her.

She turned to me, the corner of her lips pulling into a slight smile. "Thank you," she whispered.

I reached out and took her hand, my fingers intertwining with hers. "You are most welcome, dear."

I had told her we would not dally, or stray from what we came to do. No distractions or unnecessary time spent above that might risk her life, but–

But how could we not wander a bit from my usual spot? How could we not enjoy what little time we had to gather my herbs, slipping off my trail and exploring what else the world might have to offer?

She had earned it.

So we walked. We ducked under limbs and snuck through brambles. Our laughter filled the air, joining in with the songbirds that flitted overhead as they enjoyed the last moments of daylight.

And before I knew it, the sun had set. Darkness stretched across the sky and the moon came out of hiding, casting her soft light across the world around us. The triumph of night did not stop us, though, we barely noticed it.

We continued our trek through the woods, and the weightless bag at my side fell to the back of my mind. I had completely forgotten our reason for coming above in the first place.

Another push through thick bushes and brush had us both stumbling into a large clearing. My eyes raked across the field in front of us, and fell on a large lake. Moonlight reflected on the still surface of the water, making it look like glass.

"That is beautiful."

My eyes flicked to Medusa and lingered before falling back on the dark lake. "I didn't even know this was here."

Her fingers tightened around mine, and suddenly the air around us shifted from light and comfortable, to tense. Unease trickled down my spine and the hair on my arms raised.

"You've never been this far?" she asked.

I shook my head slightly, surveying the treeline surrounding the clearing. Something was watching us from the shadows. My carelessness crashed down on me, and the realization of what I had done hit me forcefully.

"No," I whispered. "We should probably turn back."

A large screech owl burst through the trees. We jumped, clutching each other tightly. He landed in a branch nearby and chuffed loudly. My stomach settled and my body relaxed.

I huffed a nervous laugh. "It was just an owl."

"He is huge," she said, her snakes' heads bobbing up and down to get a good look at him.

With the uncomfortable feeling I had before now at ease, we nestled down by the waters edge. Moonlight hung high in the sky, the peaceful sound of crickets and frogs called out, and somehow, I lost track of the time.

We might have stayed there all night, had it not been for the long string of yawning from Medusa. Her snakes struggled to keep their eyes open, and she was all but curled in my lap. Her voice was soft, her words coming more slowly.

"I think it's time we go back," I said.

I didn't want to suggest it, again; to tear her away from the place she obviously loved so much. It was different– seeing her in the mortal lands. She moved through it all like she belonged there.

Because she did.

All that could have been for her was ripped out of her hands, her life and her old self stripped away like the shed of a snake. Though there was sadness in my heart for all she had lost, there was a selfish piece of me that was thankful for it. I would not have her, if all that happened had not transpired.

"I am rather tired." I could hear the conflict in her voice. She did not want to leave.

"We'll come back soon. It seems we did not find a single thing we came for, anyway."

Her face turned up to me, and she did not need eyes for me to see the light and hope she felt. "You promise?"

With a finger under her chin, I brought her lips to mine. My heart fluttered and my stomach flipped. I would never get used to it.

"Yes, Medusa. I promise."

Because, as I was reminded time and time again, she could have anything she wanted from me. I would go to the ends of the earth for her. All she had to do was say the word, and I would act without a second thought.

The Fates had gifted me with something far more powerful than any magic or spell I could cast. Something I never dreamed I would have.

They had brought Medusa into my life, and in doing so they had given me love.

Pure, unadulterated love.

And I would do everything within my means to hold onto it.

26.

Two of Swords

I closed the door to Medusa's small home softly. She was sleeping soundly in her bed, the excitement of the day spent gallivanting above had worn her to the bone. I was nowhere near tired, though. Sleep had surrendered in its struggle to take me, and left me with wide eyes and a clear mind.

I took several steps into the iron wastes of the underworld and paused to really take it in for the first time in a long while. It seemed much darker after being in the mortal lands. Even the moonlight had granted the illusion that nightfall was not as endless as I remembered.

Or perhaps I had been too distracted.

I lifted my palms to the gray sky and allowed my magic to swallow me. I appeared outside of my hut, trying to avoid startling the animals inside, and my eyes fell on a note stuck to the door. It was folded and sealed with wax, but the ornate nature of my name scrawled along the front told me immediately who it was from.

I snatched the letter from the door and ripped it open. The contents inside were no surprise.

Witch,

Please come to the manor. Take note of the fact I instructed Hermes to leave this letter outside of your residence, instead of tracking you down.

~ Hades

P.S. - Don't forget the apple pie.

"He thinks he's funny," I mumbled, crumpling the paper in my fist.

Even though I knew exactly why he was summoning me, I would go to the manor. The thought of him being dragged from his sleep to argue with me again might have played a part in my decision.

Either way, he was getting what he asked for.

***

I banged on the iron door to the manor, my other hand balancing a large pie, as he requested. Long moments of silence stretched by as I waited for someone to answer. Just as I was about to shove the door and enter on my own, it swung open.

He was not in nightclothes, as I expected. Nor were his red eyes full of exhaustion or sleep. He wore a button down shirt, and his hair was pulled back into a low bun. A shadow of a beard covered his jawline. He looked worse for wear than he had since the last time I saw him.

"You look like shit," I said, pushing my way past him.

"You're late," he muttered, closing the door behind me.

I turned on my heel, my brows furrowed and a snarl already threatening to pull the corner of my lips down. "I do not recall there being a time set on your little love note."

He rolled his eyes and strode past me, making his way to the dining hall. "The pie smells good," he said over his shoulder.

I fought back the urge to drop it on the marble floor, and followed him further into the manor. The table was set, as it always was, with empty plates and cups. Every blasted candle the man seemed to own was burning, like he was trying to chase away the darkness of the Underworld.

That was impossible, though. I was not sure the darkness could be quelled, even if there was a sun hanging high in the gray sky above the realm. It was a ravaging, dreary darkness that seemed to emit, not only from the sky, but the iron itself.

There was surely a reason for it, some magic or power or God who brought those shadows to the world below, but that knowledge had been lost to time.

He grabbed a plate and a knife and turned to me expectantly– waiting for the pie.

Impatient.

I hurried over and set the dessert on the table, retreating a step, and watched as he cut a slice that was far larger than necessary.

"Are you going to have some?" he asked without looking at me.

I had half a mind to say no, just because I knew it would annoy him. But after smelling it for so long, it was nearly impossible to not indulge.

"Not so large a piece as you plan to gorge yourself on."

He shot me a sidelong glance, but did not respond as he cut a small sliver and slid it to me. It was too small, which he had obviously done on purpose, but spite held my tongue and I accepted it silently.

We sat at the table, and several moments passed as we ate quietly. The air was thick with a building tension, as the impending argument lingered over my head. I knew why he asked me to come, and my answer had not changed from the last time we spoke.

"I need you to go above," he finally said.

I set my fork down abruptly and it clattered against the plate. The sound was harsh against the stillness of the manor, and echoed along the mostly empty space.

"How many times must we do this, Hades? I will not go above and tirelessly search for this alleged Goddess, and even if I were to stumble across her at some point– I would not bring her here."

He slid his nearly empty plate away and his eyes lifted to mine. "I am not asking anymore, Hecate."

I recoiled. "Excuse me?"

He sat back and folded his arms. "You're right. You are stubborn. We could do this dance over and over, and you will not change your mind. I did not want to have to do this–"

"Hades…" I slid my seat back and stood. In all our years bickering and fighting he had never–

"*I* am the king of this place. *I* rule the Underworld. If you and your Gorgon wish to stay here, you'll do as I say."

He was *threatening* me.

"You wouldn't dare."

He pushed himself up to his feet and glared at me. "I have asked nicely, but I will not keep doing this forever. You will either go above and search for the Goddess, or you and your friend can find yourselves at the mercy of someone else."

"She has nowhere to go!"

My voice rang out, shrill and desperate. Perhaps it was that which gave him pause, or it was the fear in my eyes. Medusa could not go above again. She would be hunted for the rest of her days by those who did not understand, and she was unwelcome in Olympus. The Underworld was her only chance at a peaceful life.

"You cannot do this," I continued, tears brimming my eyes. "You know she was forced here, despite your kindness on the matter. If it were feasible to take her above to live, we would already be there. She yearns for the mortal realm, Hades. How do you think your Goddess of Spring will feel once she's snatched and taken here? She will hate you."

145

I saw uncertainty flash across his face. "You don't understand–"

"Don't I? You see her as an object you deserve. She is not some faceless, nameless doll, Hades! She is– or will be– a living, breathing Goddess. She will be crafted especially for the sun, and the flowers. She will be soft. This place will break her."

He shook his head. "You don't know that. The Fates–"

"Listen to yourself! You sound just like your brothers."

Flames erupted from the floor and heat blazed from around him, causing me to blink. "Enough!"

I lifted my chin. "You know I'm right."

The fire weakened to little more than embers, but his eyes still burned. "What you think of me does not matter. You'll go above, Witch. I'll not say it again."

"You say what I think does not matter, but your outburst says otherwise." I turned on my heel and stormed toward the exit.

He would not force us out. His temper was hot, and he lashed out occasionally, but he was not cruel. I would call his bluff, and stand my ground.

I was not going to be his puppet.

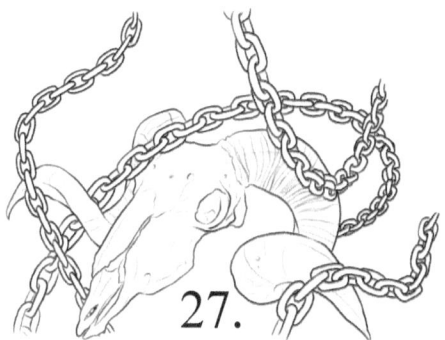

27.

The Devil

Darkness was everywhere. It surrounded me, pressed tightly against my body, filling my eyes and my nose like a rushing river. It was frigid as a river, as well, causing me to shake uncontrollably. I could not see nor hear a thing, as if the darkness had swallowed everything else around me.

Pain shot through my head, like someone was probing my brain with their fingers. I winced and fought against the urge to yell out, then squinted against the shadows.

Where was I?

A soft, cool light flared, cutting through all of the black smoke. The glow struggled against it, flicking and weaving through– like it was searching. Yet, every time it found a place where it could burn a little brighter, the darkness took it again.

I lifted my hands near my face. The light was just strong enough as it moved that I could barely see my fingers through the smoke. No matter how many times I turned, or how hard I strained my eyes, there was nothing more to see.

It should have panicked me. My heart should have been racing and full of dread, yet...

Instead, I found myself curious. I took a step, my movements slowed by the thick shadows around me.

"Who is there?" My words rippled and distorted to the point they could not be recognized.

A moment of silence passed, and then a voice sounded. It was deep and rumbling, but impossible to trace. "The Keeper of Keys," it said. "My, how long I've searched for you."

The key around my neck grew white hot and I hissed, ripping it free. It dangled in my hands, still at first. Then it swung in slow, deliberate circles.

"Speak, Titan. Do not leave me bereft at our first meeting."

My stomach sank as the oily feeling of Chaos seeped into me. It was not possible. Chaos was an immaterial power, a being with no body– it should not be able to speak.

The key froze in the air to my left and I turned. All I could see was darkness. Then the key moved, slowly pointing in front of me. My heart dropped like a heavy stone. I glanced up from the key into the darkness– into Chaos.

"What do you want from me?" My tone was far more clipped than it should have been in the presence of such an entity. Perhaps I was too brazen– or too stupid.

He laughed, the sound echoing around me. "There are many things you have to offer, Moon Mistress."

"There is nothing I wish to offer you, Chaos. Let me go." I should not have spoken to it through gritted teeth. I should not have raised my voice at it.

The darkness swelled, pressing against me harder, and the soft glow of light was nearly strangled out by it. "You took from me, and you offer nothing in return?"

His anger should have been enough to shut me up, to bring me to my knees to beg. Instead, I stood my ground.

The key shifted, pointing behind me and I whirled around. "You forced that power on me– I did not ask for it."

He barked a laugh. "Yet, you used it freely. You did not refuse it."

"I had no choice–"

"There is always a choice." His voice dripped in my ear. "Sometimes they are easy to make, sometimes they are difficult, and sometimes we regret them. But always, dear Maiden, there is a choice."

My mouth became dry, and I found myself at a loss for words. I was a captive in his darkness with nowhere to go, no way to escape. "And what choice is this, then? You give me no option but to offer something in return for the power I did not want."

"Your choice," he said slowly, "is offer something in return for the power of mine you used, or stay here with me. It gets quite lonely here."

"It is not a choice if you are forcing my hand!" I snapped.

He laughed again. "I am forcing no one's hand. I would gladly accept your company."

"Neither of the options you give me are appealing."

"A hard choice is still that. It is your decision to make."

Defeat closed in on me. I could see no way out without giving him something in return. "And what sort of thing could I offer someone such as yourself? What am I compared to you?"

"You discredit yourself, Hecate. You are older and wiser than most. And stronger. Offer me your body so that I may walk the world once more. Offer me your power, or your key. Offer me refuge in your mind when I wish it."

My fists clenched. "It sounds like what you really seek is freedom."

He did not respond.

The glow of light found weakness in his hesitance and flared brightly, cutting through the darkness and chasing it away from me. He growled and yelled, fighting for control again.

"Go!" the light called out. The voice was soft and feminine. "Leave this place!"

With a force unlike anything I had seen before I was thrust out of his realm. I jolted up, sweat dripping down my body, my breathing ragged. The darkness around me stole my breath and without thinking I lifted my hand and summoned a small fire in my palm.

I was in bed. The dogs were sitting up, staring at me. Galinthias and Hecuba were laying at the foot of the bed, their eyes drilling into me.

"It was not a dream," I said. I was unsure if I was speaking to them or reassuring myself.

The oily feeling lingered on my skin, as did the pressure of the shadows pushing against me. I threw my covers off and slipped from my bed, ripping the thick curtains away from the window to let the soft light of the Underworld into my room.

I had no idea who the voice was that had saved me, and no idea if Chaos would come back for me again. That was a matter for me to deal with when I was more clear headed. I needed–

I threw on a robe and my boots, then kissed the top of Hecuba's head. "I'll be back."

I needed Medusa.

28.

Five of Cups

I appeared outside of her home in a plume of purple smoke. The oily power that belonged to Chaos did not force itself on me, but it was there– hiding in wait.

My heart thundered, pounding in my ears as I reached up and banged on the door.

"Please," I whispered.

If I had to spend another minute alone, I thought I might lose my sanity entirely.

Her footsteps on the wooden floorboards rose above my heart, and I sighed in relief. She cracked the door and she gasped. The next second she was swinging it open wide.

"Hecate? It is so early. Are you–"

I dove into her arms, cutting her off. Tears streamed down my face. Her hands wrapped around me without hesitation and she held me close. Finally, my racing heart slowed and my breathing became even. All of the fear and adrenaline from my meeting with Chaos fell away.

"What on earth has happened?" she asked softly.

"It will not make much sense to you, I'm afraid," I mumbled into her shoulder.

She ran her fingers through my hair, her other hand pressed against the small of my back. "I needn't understand– just to be here to listen."

That– that was the reason she had infiltrated my rotten heart and transformed its nature; the reason she had made me feel things I never thought possible.

I pulled away and took her face in my hands. "You are a darling little thing, did you know that?"

She smiled brightly, flashing pointed fangs at me. "So I've heard." Her hands found mine and she dragged me into the small cabin. "Come. Let us get comfortable and you can tell me what is plaguing you."

Her home was well-lit with candles, the curtains pulled back to allow as much light in as possible. Steeped tea clung to the air, leaving a bitter, earthy smell filling the rooms. She led me to her bedchamber and sat me on the edge of the bed.

She knelt at my feet and grabbed my boots, and I pulled away. "Hells, Medusa, I can remove my own boots."

"You are shaken. Just let me do it– you can relax."

Overbearing and mothering. That was what she was. In prior years, I might have found that a bothersome thing, but with her... With her it warmed my heart.

153

My boots hit the ground with a loud thud. She left them where they fell, and crawled into the bed beside me, snuggling us both under the furred covers.

"Now," she said sweetly, "what has happened."

I mulled over what had transpired with Chaos and the unnamed light. She would not even know who I was talking about, the Gods had erased nearly all that happened before their reign. But to start at the beginning would be a far grander, far more convoluted tale than I intended to tell.

"There were others– before the Gods that are in power today. Beings more powerful, and more cruel. They were stripped of their rule, overthrown by Zeus and the others."

Her brows furrowed, and my eyes slid across the scars on her face. It seemed an insult to say such a thing about the beings before the current reign of Gods; to say those that caused her such pain were nothing in comparison.

But it was true.

"The first God that came into existence, as far as my knowledge anyway, was Chaos. He birthed most of the next generation, the Titans. Not in the way that you may be used to– but still. Anyway, he was robbed of his physical form in the war that came at the start of Zeus' rule."

She listened intently, her snakes nestled down and stared at me. Memories of the war and the carnage that came with it flooded me, and I reached out to take her hand in mine.

"The belief is that one day our long lives will expire, and we will all return to Chaos."

As I quieted, lost to the memories and the fear of the future, she spoke. "So where does that lead us to today?"

154

I had gone off track, as I suspected. There was too much information to give her all at once. "I met Chaos today," I said.

She frowned and her head tilted. "You... met him?"

"Yes. He's a gem of a man, really. Quite like you might expect for God who was overthrown and stripped of nearly everything he had."

"Are you alright?" Her snakes' eyes scanned over me. "You aren't hurt?"

"No." I paused. "I used his power, accidentally, not terribly long ago. It seems he believes I owe him for it."

She shifted beside me, her nervousness tangible. "What does he want?"

I glanced over at her. It would not matter how I phrased it. There was no gentle way to say what he wanted. "He is trying to find a way to be freed from his prison. He wants a physical form."

She sat upright. "*Your* physical form?"

I laughed, though really, it was not funny at all. "I do not think he cares who the body comes from, or if it is an entirely new body crafted especially for him."

"What did you tell him?"

"I was ripped free of him before we could reach an agreement."

Her brows pulled together. "Ripped free of him?"

I shook my head. "I could not break loose myself, but there was someone there with him. A woman, I think."

"Well, I am thankful to whoever it was. Do you think he will come after you again?"

I leaned my head against her shoulder. "I have no doubt about it. He will definitely try again, and if I am alone with him next time... I'm not sure what I'll be able to do about it."

Silence fell over the room as the gravity of my situation loomed over us.

"Can you ask Hades to help?"

I sat up and looked at her. "After I refused his request for help? No, I think not. That will only give him more leverage against me."

She sighed. "Surely we can figure something out."

"I'm afraid this is the game, Dear One. The Gods are only after what might bring them the most gain, regardless of who it hurts in the process."

She smiled sadly. "You are not like that."

I leaned in and kissed her forehead. "Oh, but I am. It just so happens that *you* are the most I can gain."

She brought my hand up and kissed my palm. "You are far kinder than you give yourself credit for."

I took her face in my hands and brushed a soft kiss on her lips. "I am every bit as angry and vengeful as the others. Rotten and spoiled to my core."

She shook her head. "I do not believe that for a second."

I sat back, looking up at the ceiling. "I hope you always view me in such a way."

But she wouldn't. There would come a day when she would see my true colors and recoil from me. The Gods had a way of ruining things, and contrary to her belief, I was no exception.

The Fates had tried to bring light into my life once before, and I had taken it for granted; squandered it. I would have to pay for the way I raised Circe one day.

"We should do something to take your mind off of things for a while," she said.

A smile crept across my face and I rolled on top of her. "Oh? And what did you have in mind?"

She laughed, bright and carefree. My lips met hers, then traveled down her neck.

"I was thinking," she said between heavy breaths and soft moans, "that we could go above again."

I stopped at the neckline of her dress and looked up at her. "You want to go to the mortal realm again, already?"

She smiled sheepishly, a pink hue overtaking her green cheeks. "I thought we could go back to that lake. Maybe we could go in? I have not swam in so long."

I nodded slowly. Perhaps she was right– a little time without worry and political games would do me well. Whatever was going to happen with Chaos, would happen. Sitting around, worried and full of anxiety, would change nothing.

If he was going to torment me, I might as well enjoy what time I had without him. I could make a plan for how to deal with him later, after I had time to clear my mind and reset myself.

"Very well, then," I said. "To the mortal realm, we go."

'There is always a choice.'

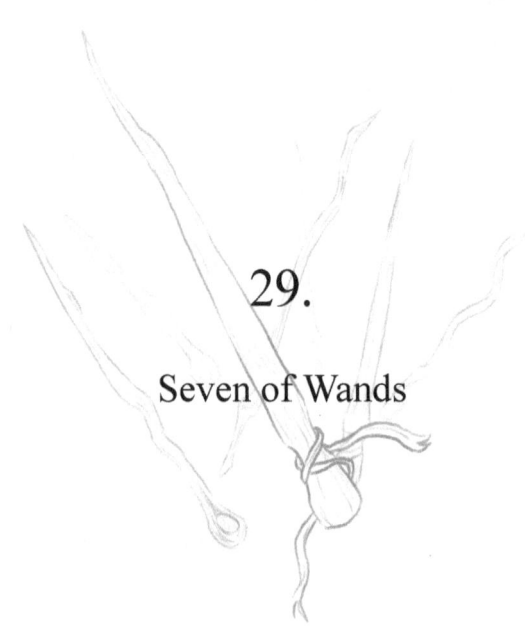

29.

Seven of Wands

Medusa's steps were confident– more at ease with our journey the second time around. To my surprise, she was nearly leading the way through the tunnels. One trip from the Underworld to the mortal realm and she had almost memorized the entire route.

We crossed into the land of the living, startled once more by the bats, with our hearts much lighter and a joyous laughter on our tongues. Chaos had slipped my mind, the time spent with Medusa smothered the memory of him.

It was late by the time we reached the lake. The screech owl had perched in a tree high above us, and the moon had found her place in the sky, surrounded by millions of stars. Crickets and frogs sang into the night, filling the cool air with music.

Medusa settled down in the grass at the edge of the water. "This is the most beautiful place I have ever been."

The wonder in her voice brought a smile to my face. She was the one, truly perfect thing to ever exist. I wanted to freeze that moment; to capture it in a bottle and keep it close to me forever.

I sat down next to her, my eyes raking across the curves of her soft face. "Every ray of light the moon casts, every twinkle from each star, every drop in this lake– they pale in comparison to you."

She shook her head, her cheeks flushing. "You cannot compare me to the moon."

"I can, and I will. And she will fall short every time."

Her face turned to me and the corner of her lips pulled up into a slight smile. "You cannot possibly mean that."

I glanced up at the sky, then my eyes flicked to Medusa again. "I do mean it."

Hells below, she intoxicated me– muddled my mind in a way that made me feel somehow so small, yet so large all at the same time. Like I was nothing more than a speck, but still, unstoppable.

Perhaps that was what destroyed all of my apprehension and allowed me to open myself up to her so completely– allowed the words I said next to fly from my lips without a second thought.

"I love you."

Her brows rose and her jaw dropped. In the second it took her to reply, I had already cursed myself for being so careless, and considered how I might flee from her and bury myself beneath the rubble of a mountain.

Before I had the chance to act on my shame, she took my face in her hands and brought my lips to hers. When she pulled away, she was smiling.

"I love you, too. I'm not sure how I ever lived without you, before."

I kissed her again, grabbing her hips to pull her onto my lap. Our breath mingled as our hands roved each other's bodies, soft moans filling the air between each kiss.

Her fingers tangled in my hair, and a gasp left my lips as she gave a sudden yank, craning my head back. She kissed down my neck, sending a wave of fire through me, just beneath my skin. An ache built between my legs, and my nails dug into her thighs, urging her on.

She pulled my dress off my shoulders, kissing down toward my breasts. I fumbled with the hem of her dress, exposing soft skin, and my hand slipped between her legs. My fingers made small circles, and she ground down on my hand, her lips crashing into mine.

I was sure of one thing: I loved her. She would be my one and only for the rest of our lives. Nothing else in my life mattered. She was the reason my heart beat in my chest.

She laid her hand on my shoulder and gently pushed me back until I was laying on the ground. I grabbed fistfulls of grass as she lifted my dress and her tongue swirled, her fingers pumping in and out of me. I was not new to sex. In fact, I had several partners over my long life, but never had anyone dragged me to the edge in the way she did.

Her name was on my tongue as a wave of ecstasy crashed over me. Then her lips were on mine again. With our legs tangled we moved against each other, climbing toward another climax.

My senses had been swallowed by her. Her scent, her moans, the feel of her core grinding against mine. Everything else around us faded into the abyss.

As one, we cried out, then crumpled into each other. She heaved several ragged breaths and then huffed a laugh. A smile fell over me, and I kissed her cheek and neck.

"I love you," I said again.

She brushed her thumb over my bottom lip. "And I love you, my darling enchantress."

I shook my head, but I could not fight the smile from my face. "Do not patronize me."

She said something else. I knew because I saw her lips move, but her voice did not reach my ears. Instead, a shrill scream echoed in my head. It was a familiar voice– the woman who had saved me from Chaos.

I did not intend to move my arms; to shove Medusa off of me, onto the ground. My body moved on its own, by pure instinct, or perhaps the unnamed woman controlled me.

Regardless, Medusa tumbled to the ground, and I rolled after her. I looked up in time to see a flash of metal as a sword was swung down, the blade burying deep into the earth where Medusa and I had been just seconds before.

A helm hit the ground with a loud thump. I knew the helm well. It had been used to help win the war between Gods and Titans long ago.

It belonged to Hades.

30.

Seven of Swords

My eyes darted up to his face.

The man before us was not Hades, though the helm was indeed his. His features were contorted with anger. He wielded a long sword in one hand, and a shield in the other. I knew the shield as well. It was Athena's.

My brows furrowed, and I shoved myself up to my feet. My arms were outstretched, blocking him from Medusa. I did not recognize the man. He was muscled but young.

He darted around me, moving much faster than a human should be able to, and that was when I saw them– the winged sandals Hermes sometimes wore.

I shot a blast of dark magic out at him, knocking him back onto the ground. "What do you want?" I shouted.

He pushed himself up quickly and lifted his sword and shield. "I've no qualms with you, Witch. I've come for Gorgon's head."

My heart dropped, and my eyes flicked between the sandals, the shield, and the helm. They had come together behind my back; made a pact to take Medusa's life and destroy mine.

Anger, black as the iron of the Underworld, coursed through my veins. My sight rippled and blurred and pain shot through me as power grew and pulled at the seams that held it in place.

"Excuse me?" My voice came in a symphony.

"Please, miss. I do not wish to fight you. I just want the monster."

"Monster?" My voice rumbled and echoed. "I see only one monster here."

But that was a lie. There were two monsters standing at the edge of the water, and neither of them were Medusa. I glanced over my shoulder at her. She was on her hands and knees, her dress disheveled and her snakes pulling and hissing as if they might flee somewhere to safety.

"I have no choice," the young man said. "It must be this way."

I would tear Olympus and the Underworld apart. I would bring the mortal realm to ruins. The Gods were either ignorant or needlessly confident if they thought they could take her from me.

I lifted my hand, pulling power free from its cage, and sent a whip toward him. He ducked and ran out of the way, dodging only due to the sandals from Hermes.

"I do not know who sent you, but I am giving you one more chance, child. Leave this place."

Fear flashed across his face, and I could see he was torn. Still, he dug his heels into the ground and gripped his sword tighter. He would not heed my warning.

"Very well," I snarled.

Black tentacles shot out from the ground at my feet, lashing out at him in a flurry. He slashed at them with his sword, and the blade cut through my magic. His weapon had been enchanted– under the command of which God, I could not have said.

He darted forward, weaving between my magic, cutting it down as he went. I raised my hands to ward him off, but he dropped, sliding under my arm with his sword ready to swing.

Straight for Medusa.

I whirled around as he jumped to his feet and drew the weapon over his head. She let out a garbled sound, primal and full of terror, as she threw herself back. The sword swung down as she scrambled backward. The way the blade came down was much more careless than he had been before, his aim far off mark.

It dug into the ground and he grunted, pulling it free once more. I watched as he sliced it through the air again–

In the opposite direction that she had moved to.

Confusion settled over her face as she sat with her mouth ajar. He whirled, swinging the sword haphazardly. She turned to me and shook her head slightly.

A smile spread across my face.

He had his eyes closed.

The poor boy had no idea the Gorgon he sought had been maimed and left unable to turn him to stone. Probably because I was the only God who knew about it.

My magic swallowed me and I appeared behind him. With a swift motion, dark power swirled around my arm and shaped into a solid point aimed at his heart.

"No!" Medusa screamed.

The man spun toward us and his elbow caught my jaw, knocking me back. Then he was charging at Medusa again, his shield covering his face, sword drawn.

Oh, I wanted to be angry with her. She had ruined my chance at ending his life and saving hers.

But I could not.

Her kindness had played a part in softening me. It was one of the many reasons I loved her. How could I then turn around and be outraged by it?

I lifted my arms and shot a blast of magic at him, sending him flying to the ground. Medusa took the chance to push herself up, and she ran to me, diving into my arms. I held her close, darkness swirling around our feet.

She hated the magic of the Gods, I knew that, and it made me hesitate, my power faltering long enough for him to orient himself. Once more, he was rushing us– ready to cleave his weapon down.

The man was determined, I would give him that.

Power swallowed us and we appeared several feet behind him.

"I have no choice, Medusa," I said to her.

"You cannot kill him," she begged.

He turned and charged again. Someone would not be leaving that field. Someone would die that night. The moon in the sky would bear witness to spilled blood, and the decision of whose life was stolen was mine, and mine alone.

I would have to break a pact with the God of the Dead. Not that it mattered, seeing as he had given his helm of invisibility to the man sent to kill Medusa. Whatever the cost was of breaking his rules, I would deal with it later.

My eyes lifted to the night sky, and I sent out a silent apology to the death I was about to bring about. I did not like killing needlessly, especially those who did not deserve it.

And Medusa might hate me for it. She might never forgive me.

But I was left with no choice.

I grabbed the key from around my neck and ripped it loose, dangling it in the air in front of me. An ancient language rolled off my tongue, my vision blurring again, and white, hot light erupted from the key.

Darkness came after it. A black hole that ripped through realms– a door straight to the Underworld.

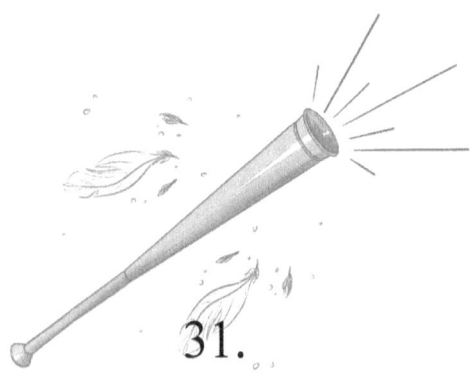

31.

Judgment

Medusa gripped me tightly, her nails digging into my arms as her snakes stared into the black hole. The man had halted, frozen in place as he, too, looked into the portal between realms.

I shouted in the ancient tongue– an order, a command. She would heed me, not knowing what would befall her.

A loud thump broke the silence that had fallen over the forest as a copper leg stepped through the door and slammed into the earth. Two thin hands reached out, gripping the edges of the pathway from the Underworld, and she heaved herself into the mortal realm.

Her skin was a pale green, shimmering scales covering her body. A tangled mess of snakes sat atop her head. She let out an ear shattering scream, hurling herself toward the young man.

He yelled, taking a step back, then steeled himself. With his eyes squeezed shut he drew the sword back and charged the beast I had summoned.

I did not wait to see him slay her; to watch as he sliced the head from her shoulders and took it as a trophy. I grabbed Medusa's arm and shoved her through the dark portal into the Underworld, leaving the man to finish the job he came for.

As we appeared on the other side, I closed the pathway between realms and shoved the key into the pocket of my dress. Medusa turned toward me, confusion and anger clear in her face.

"What have you done? Who was that?"

I stormed past her, my boots crunching on iron. "An Empusa–a demon from the Underworld."

She ran to catch up, grabbing my arm to stop me. "That was another Gorgon!" Her voice was shrill.

"No!" I shouted, whirling to face her. She stopped dead in her tracks. "That was an Empusa. I commanded her to shift into the form of a Gorgon to take your place."

She retreated a step, her mouth falling open slightly. She pressed a hand flat against her chest, looking as though she were about to faint. "You sent her to die?"

It took everything in me not to yell again. I was just as outraged and upset with the situation as she was. Sending the Empusa to her death was not something I ever wanted to do.

"He would have kept coming for you. We had two options; kill him, or allow him to kill something he perceived to be a Gorgon. You asked me not to kill him, that left me with no choice–"

"There is always a choice!" Her voice was cracked and sharp, but it was her choice in words that knocked the air from my lungs.

168

The same words that Chaos had said to me.

"What did you say?" I whispered.

She paused, her brows furrowed. "I said there is always a choice. That poor creature did not deserve to die! Just because you're a God does not give you the right to make such a decision–"

My mouth dried. "Why would you say that?"

"Because there had to be another way for us to handle this. Surely we could have done something to–"

"*There is always a choice.* That is what Chaos said to me when he demanded a price for the power of his that I used."

She flinched, a grimace falling over her face. "I'm sorry, Hecate. I didn't know…"

Of course she didn't. She couldn't have.

My anger melted away and I stepped toward her, pulling her into my arms. "Hate me, if you must, but you are what matters most to me. I will not let you be killed, even if it means allowing someone else to die. If I had seen another way, I would not have done it."

Slowly, her arms wrapped around me and her shoulders shook. "I do not want to be the reason someone loses their life."

"I'm sorry." I meant it. Hurting her was the last thing I wanted.

She pulled away and took my face in her hands. "I am not mad at you. I just… I don't understand why he was after me to begin with."

I paused, staring at her, as I contemplated telling her what I had learned from the items he carried. She must have seen the look on my face, because she took a step back and frowned.

"What is it? What do you know?"

I sighed. "The shield he carried was from Athena, the sandals were from Hermes, and the helm belonged to Hades."

She shook her head. "No. That cannot be right. Athena, I understand, but why would Hermes and Hades..." Her voice trailed off.

I reached out and patted her cheek. "I plan to find out why they took part in that, Dear One, and remedy it immediately."

She grabbed my wrist. "Perhaps we should forget this happened."

My brows furrowed and a frown pulled at my lips. "Why in the Hells would we do that?"

Her chin trembled. "Don't confront them. I don't want you to get hurt or get in trouble."

I smiled at her, my face softening. "Oh, darling. Do not fret yourself over me. I will be fine."

"But–"

"Go to my cabin and sit with Hecuba. I'm going to talk to Hades. I promise–" I kissed her cheek. "I will be fine."

I turned and summoned another portal. One that led straight to Hades' manor. "I love you," I called over my shoulder.

"I love you, as well," she said as I stepped into the darkness and disappeared.

There was no question in my mind why Hades had given the man his helm; no question why he had aided Athena. It was a message to me, a punishment for not following his command regarding the Goddess of Spring.

He wanted to teach me a lesson.

All he had done, instead, was send me into a fit of rage I might never escape from. I would never forgive him for what he had done.

Long gone was any chance of the two of us mending the relationship we once had.

32.

Knight of Swords

When I stepped through the other side, I was in his sitting room. I had never barged into his home unannounced before, and as my eyes fell on the Nymph straddling him, I was reminded of why.

His eyes widened and he scrambled to pull her dress down over her ass to cover her. "What the fuck are you doing, Hecate?"

"You conniving bastard!" I spat.

I sent a blast of magic at him, but he vanished before it made contact, both he and the Nymph appearing on the other side of the room. A split second before I shot another blast at him, he whisked the Nymph away in a plume of black smoke.

He deflected my attack, and it crashed into a large vase, shattering it. "What is wrong with you?" he shouted.

It only angered me more. He had some nerve to give the man his helm, but to deny it? Oh, that was even more outrageous.

"Don't play stupid!"

I sent blast after blast at him and he deflected them all as he marched toward me. My attacks became frantic, my aim off as tears stung my eyes.

Sure, the two of us had our differences and we argued, but to help Medusa be killed? It was too far. He had gone too far.

He snatched my wrists, and he shook me. "Enough! Tell me what the Hells is going on."

Something in his voice broke me. I let out a strangled sob and my knees gave out from under me. I hit the floor and tears broke free.

Medusa had nearly died. I had nearly lost her.

He knelt in front of me and lifted my face to his. "Hecate?"

"You tried to have her killed!" I screamed. "You tried to take her from me!"

His brows furrowed. "What are you talking about?"

"Don't try to deny it. He had your helm!"

Hades frowned, and had the audacity to look confused. "Hecate, I have given my helm to no one. It sits in my office, hidden away."

"You lie!" It could not be true. I saw the helm with my own eyes.

He flinched and withdrew his hand. "I am not lying to you. The helm is here, where it has been for ages. No one has touched it."

I shook my head.

A heavy sigh left his lips. "Must I show you the helm to prove my innocence? I still do not even understand what has happened."

I shoved myself to my feet. "The man you and Athena sent to kill Medusa! He had her shield and your helm."

Hades stood and folded his arms. "Why would I send someone to kill her, or aid in any way, after I gave her refuge here? What purpose would that serve me?"

"You did it to force me to go above to look for your precious Goddess!" I snarled.

His eyebrow arched and the muscle in his jaw ticked. Silence fell over the room as he stood still and rigid.

I was right. There was no other reason why he would have done it.

"Medusa lives?" he asked slowly, like he was choosing his words carefully. He did not even try to deny it again.

"Yes. I sent an Empusa to die in her place," I snarled.

He tilted his head and anger flashed across his red eyes. "An Empusa? Where did this man attack you?"

I knew where he was going with his question. "The mortal realm," I said flatly.

His lip curled slightly. "And how did the Empusa get to the mortal realm?"

I slammed my palms into his chest and he took a step back. "I sent her there to die!"

His anger flared and heat radiated off of him. "You know that is strictly prohibited. The beasts of the Underworld are not to leave this realm."

"I don't care about your rules." I wiped my cheek on the back of my hand.

"You're about to care about my rules," he gritted.

"Is that so?"

173

He took a step toward me and I retreated. "You will go above and find the Goddess of Spring and bring her to me, or I will deliver your precious Gorgon to Athena on a silver platter."

In one swift motion, I drew back and slapped his face. I was backed into a corner– I had no choice but to do what he said, but I did not have to do it quietly.

He moved so quickly I barely had time to react. His hand was around my throat, holding firm but not choking me. "Keep testing me, Witch."

"You claim you want your Goddess so badly, yet the Nymph still warms your lap," I sneered. "Your Goddess will hate you, just as the rest of the world does."

I half expected him to snap my neck right there, but instead, fire erupted from him. It singed my clothes and set his furniture and art ablaze. The flames licked my skin, and the smell of burnt flesh hit my nose.

The fire disappeared as quickly as it came, but the aftermath of his outburst remained. My skin healed over quickly, but the pain lingered. He released my throat and took a step back.

"You can come back to visit your Gorgon, but I expect you to spend as much of your time above as you spend below. I want that Goddess."

I shook my head. "Very well, *Zeus*, I'll do your bidding and fetch your whore."

I gave him no time to respond or lash out once more before I vanished from his manor.

When my power dissipated and I was standing in my home, I fell to the ground again. I would go above, as he demanded. I would spend my time torn between the Underworld and the mortal realm, but I would not search for his Goddess. I would put myself as far from Demeter's grove as I could. Another continent, perhaps.

My final act of betrayal as I did what I could to keep Medusa safe.

 # 33.

The Empress

I was not standing in the darkness Chaos had wrapped me in before, but instead a lush green forest. Grass and flowers were thick under my feet, and a blue sky stretched above me.

I blinked, my hand raised to block the brightness from my eyes.

"Hello, Moon Mistress," a soft, feminine voice said.

I knew that voice. The woman from before.

My eyes flew open and my hand dropped. She stood before me, her hair falling in varying shades of brown curls down her back. Her olive skin shimmered in the sunlight. She stared at me, her eyes shifting from blue to green, then back again.

"It's you," I whispered.

Her full lips parted into a bright smile. "It is me," she said slyly, humor in her voice.

My eyes dragged down her body. Small blooms and vines were intertwined in her hair, she was wrapped in a pale green dress. Her bare feet were planted in the grass, and small flowers continued to grow and bloom all around her.

I hit my knees and tears welled in my eyes. "You are The Mother."

She smiled and nodded. "Yes, Hecate, but please– call me Gaia. There is no need for formalities."

"You saved me from Chaos."

Her face became serious. "I've done what I can, but I fear he will be back. If not to torment you, perhaps another."

That was what I had feared, anyway. It felt something I should warn the other Gods about–

But why should I, after they banded together to ruin my life?

Gaia's eyes dipped to the key around my neck, and she pressed her hand against her bosom. "I see you still carry my key."

I reached up and brushed my finger across the cool metal and it sang in response to my touch. "I've had it for as long as I can remember."

She walked over, and sat in the grass in front of me, her legs criss-crossed. "It opens portals to all of the realms, which I'm sure you have noticed. There are far more things that key can do, though."

I did not realize I was wringing my hands, until she placed hers gently on top of mine to settle me.

"What else does it do?" I asked.

She shook her head slowly, a slight grin spreading across her face. "I cannot tell you that. You must find the key's power on your own."

My face fell and my shoulders drooped. That was unfortunate. I had been in possession of the key so long already, and knew of only one ability.

"In time," she assured me. "The key chooses when to show its hand."

"You say that as though it is sentient." It seemed like a silly idea.

"In a manner of speaking," she said softly.

I glanced around the forest again. It looked exactly like the world above, except there were no signs of life there outside of the plant life. No animals, or other Gods or people.

"Where is this place?"

Her smile faded and her face became flat. "This is the land between existence." She looked at the trees and then up at the sky. "Each God's pocket of the land looks different. They all start as a clean slate, void of anything at all. After a time, it shifts, becoming whatever we wish it to be."

"Are you dead?" I dared to ask.

She laughed, and it sounded like music. "Oh no," she said. "We are not dead... Simply, locked away. There are only three beings who can truly kill a God."

My brows furrowed. "Who are they?"

"Atropos, Lachesis, and Clotho– The Moirai."

My lips parted, and I closed them again. "The Fates? The Fates can *kill* the Gods?"

178

"If they wish to. They hold the fate strings of us all. Thankfully, they are mild women. I do not think they would maliciously harm anyone."

That did not make me feel better. In fact, it made me quite nauseous. I swallowed the bile that worked its way up my throat, and clenched my fists.

"Why have you come to me?" I had many questions for her, it seemed.

She hummed, craning her head to the sky. "I suppose I just wanted to see you. You were a small babe the last time I saw you."

The stories said she helped Chaos birth all of the Titans, and some of the Gods in power after. I could not imagine why the Gods would lock her away. She was a gentle spirit, from what I could tell.

"There is another reason," she said quietly.

I tilted my head and frowned. "And that is?"

Her eyes flicked to mine, and the light blue melted to a deep green with rings of gold. "There will be another that takes my place. Guide her– teach her what you can. She will be young, and naive."

I huffed a laugh. "I do not have a good track record with raising children."

"Circe is a powerful, capable Goddess. She is kind, and nurturing. You may only see your mistakes, Hecate, but she has long forgotten them."

Tears stung my eyes. "How do you know that?"

"I see everything. Even from here."

Her words healed something broken inside me. "Who is this Goddess that is set to take your place?"

She laughed, again. It was the most melodic, enchanting sound I had ever heard. "I cannot say. You must discover that on your own, as well."

Her eyes drifted from mine and her face fell flat, like she was listening. Then she looked at me again. "It is time for you to go."

"No," I said, panic in my voice. "I have more questions."

She reached out and patted my cheek. "Believe in yourself, Hecate. Trust your instincts and your decisions. You have come far, and still further you have to go. You build a legacy in your wake. Years to come, far in the future, women everywhere will whisper your name under the moonlight. You will guide their hands and their actions long after the world denies the Gods. *You* are special."

My lip trembled. "Thank you, Gaia."

She leaned forward and pressed her lips to my forehead. "Go in peace, my sweet child."

I woke in Medusa's arms, her chest rising and falling in a rhythm. The dogs were piled onto the bed in a heap all around us, and Galinthias was nestled in my hair.

I glanced over at Hecuba, who stared at me knowingly– a twinkle in her brown eyes.

There were many things that scared me about the future, but that was a problem for later. For now, I would enjoy my time with the ones I loved.

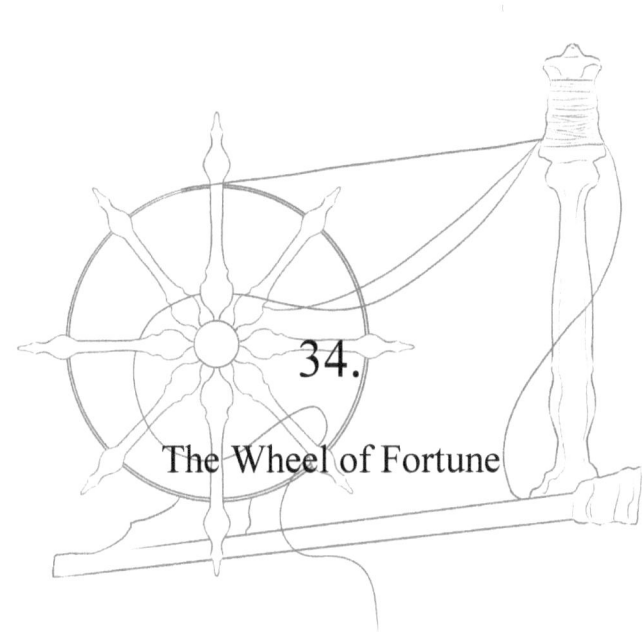

34.
The Wheel of Fortune

"Must you leave again?"

I looked up from my bag at Medusa, who held Galinthias close to her chest. "I'm afraid so. If I stay much longer, Hades may come banging on my door."

She sighed, her face falling. "I hate it when you're away. I miss you terribly."

"I miss you, as well." I leaned in and kissed her lips. "I will be back, again. There is no one that could keep me from you forever."

My words did not appear to comfort her in the slightest. "You must find his Goddess quickly. It has been years already, and you have moved dozens of times. I am ready for this to end."

181

I smiled sadly. There were not many things I kept from Medusa. Secrets were like a disease that killed you slowly, and I tried to keep as few of them as possible.

But how could I tell her I still had no intention of finding the Goddess?

"I have made no headway with the villagers," I said, clearing my throat. "There is a young woman there, though she does not have high status, she seems to run the entire place. From what I have seen, if she does not like or trust someone, the rest of the village also distrusts them. Unfortunately for me, I seem to be one of those people."

"Humans can feel a difference, you know."

I glanced up at her. "What?"

She smiled softly. "There is this… pit in your stomach when you come face to face with a God."

"I've no idea what you're talking about."

She laughed. "Because you are a God!"

I grabbed her face and kissed her again. "Do you still get a pit in your stomach when you look at me?"

"Not at all," she whispered. Her face perked up. "Who is this woman, though? Should I be concerned?"

I scoffed. "Hells, no. She is a crass woman, far too curious and prying for her own good. She drinks her tea sickeningly sweet and she argues any chance she gets. The villagers call her Fray."

Medusa chuckled. "Aside from the tea, it sounds like the two of you have quite a lot in common."

My brows knitted together and my mouth flew open. "I do not argue—" I stopped myself and narrowed my eyes at her as she smiled.

"Tell me again what the village looks like."

182

We went through it like a broken record, every place I went. Medusa wanted to hear of it in great detail. She never grew bored of my stories, and I felt sure she could recite each of them by heart, yet still, she would ask me.

"It's a quiet village, tucked in the mountains of a bright new world. The trees there are old. Older, perhaps, than the Gods themselves. Time feels frozen, and magic hangs in the air.

"The humans don't seem to notice all that lurks in the darkness, slipping between realms when the veil is thin. Their customs are ancient, things most people forgot long ago."

"And the waters?" she asked, urging me to continue.

I smiled. "The waters there are crystal clear, both the rivers and the lakes. Magic courses through their waters, just as it does their trees. Even the animals seem to sense it."

She sighed, leaning back. "It sounds magnificent."

In truth, it was a boring little place where nothing ever happened. The villagers meandered around, doing the same thing day after day. The magic and power that was nestled there went untapped and unnoticed.

But it was far from Demeter, far from any place the Gods had settled. It was the perfect spot to avoid running into the Goddess of Spring I had been sent to look for.

And for some reason, I enjoyed the silence and the monotony of it all. The only thing that could have made the village better, was if I could bring Medusa with me. I knew the way the villagers kept me at arms length, though, they would never accept her.

Medusa put Galinthias down on the floor and the little beast scurried off to find a place to hide and sleep. I wrapped my arms around Medusa as she straddled my lap.

"I really must be going," I murmured just before her lips found mine.

"Give me ten more minutes?" she begged.

"It is always ten more minutes." I was trying to scold her, but a smile tugged at my lips and my tone was soft.

"Honest, this time."

She kissed down my neck and a moan left my lips.

"Fine," I said. "Ten more minutes."

Hells to Hades and his demands. Ten minutes would make no difference at all in finding his Goddess, especially when I had no intentions on looking for her anyway.

My only concern, my only desire, was to spend every second that I could in Medusa's arms. Nothing else mattered.

She was my moon and stars, the breath in my lungs, the beat of my heart. She was my reason for waking up each day.

Nothing else mattered.

EPILOGUE

I had been in the village for years, shifting my appearance to age alongside those who lived there. My hair grayed and my skin wrinkled. Time dragged by for me as I spent my life torn between the mortal realm and the Underworld.

I only truly enjoyed myself when I was able to slip to the land below and cradle Medusa closely.

A chicken darted under my feet, running as fast as its small legs would take it, as a group of children ran after it. I watched them chase the animal, laughter flitting through the air.

I stuck my hand in my bag, feeling around for the small vials of potions I had brought to sell for food and other goods. The villagers bartered their way through life, which was well and good enough for me.

They thought me an herbalist, or a witch, not unlike the Gods, I supposed. And just as the Gods, I was wholly unwelcome, unless I had something to offer.

I glanced out toward the small community garden and my eyes locked with a child no more than four years old.

Her hair was a tangled mess of fiery curls, a splatter of freckles spread across her cheeks and nose. Her small hands had been clawing at the earth, and she was covered in dirt all the way up to her elbows.

It was none of those things, though, that kept me frozen in place. It was her wild, bright eyes. They were greener than any I had seen before, and were far wiser than any child her age should have. She looked at me like she could see straight through my glamour into my soul. Like it was the eyes of a Titan she was staring at, not the eyes of an old woman.

She pushed herself up from the ground and made for my direction, keeping her gaze on me. There was a confidence in her steps as she marched forward, ignoring the other children who parted as she walked by them. They made sure to keep their distance from her, as if she were plagued with some horrid disease.

If she noticed, I could not tell. Her attention was tunneled directly on me.

She stopped just in front of me and craned her head up to look at me, and for just a moment I was flooded with the memory of Circe. My heart cracked, nearly shattering with guilt and regret.

"Hello," the little fire-haired girl said brightly.

I found myself aching to reach out and scoop her up, to hold her tightly and never let her go. It was the heartbreak of losing Circe, I told myself.

"Hello," I said softly.

She reached out and took the hem of my dress in her small hands, rubbing the rough fabric between her filthy fingers. Any other time I might have scolded her, but not then. Then, I was filled with too many emotions, my soul raw with things that might have been.

When her eyes lifted to mine once more, she smiled. "My name is Kora."

SNEAK PEEK

Zagreus

Blood and power thrummed through my veins. It crashed and slammed against the seams that held it at bay over and over again, screaming and demanding to be set free. It knew exactly what it wanted.

My vision tunneled, a thick red veil falling over everything. I was starving– ravenous– and no matter how much I fed, it was not enough.

And the anger–

It tore and ripped through my mind, consuming any reason that lay there before. I was no longer a man or a God. I was a beast, and the hunger in my belly demanded to be fed. My mouth was watering, saliva dripping from the corner of my lips.

Before her touch, I had never felt such intense wrath; such starvation I was driven mad. I had always been quiet, and agreeable. I had prided myself on being pleasant, on being a kind soul.

But that was a thought that would haunt me later, for then– in that moment– the ability to think had fled me. Abandoned me to be swallowed by Melinoë's sick power.

She could not help it, though. It was not her fault. She was only a child. How could anyone have expected her to control such a thing? Or be stable enough while so young not to abuse it?

The coppery tang of blood filled my mouth. It dripped from my chin and my elbows as I clawed the boar beneath me apart with my bare hands. The animal writhed and bellowed, still clinging to what little life it had left.

The act would leave me nauseous for weeks; it would fill me with guilt and shame. And the screams of those around me, the ones that were drowned by the wrath and the hunger…

Those would haunt me for the rest of my life, they would stain my name forever.

But it was not Melinoë's fault.

My sister was only a child.

ACKNOWLEDGEMENTS

AND

NOTES FROM THE AUTHOR

The Gorgon and The Witch has been such a labor of love. I poured so much of my time and my heart into this project, and I will not lie and say it was easy. This book challenged my skill and required a lot of emotion, but boy was the outcome worth it!

It became apparent very early on that I wanted the theme of this book to revolve around the choices we make and the results that follow. Some choices we make feel small at the moment, but over time we realize that those small things grow and shape both our lives, and ourselves as people.

I hope that each and every one of you who made it this far managed to close the book feeling seen, heard, and like you ended with more than you began with.

The Gorgon and The Witch would absolutely not have been possible without the help of Veronica– who poured over it several times to help me with editing. Veronica, I appreciate your honesty and all of the hard work you gave so freely to help me bring this book to life! I will never be able to thank you enough.

A huge thank you to my husband, who continues to support me every step of the way, carry my heavy boxes full of books, and listen to me gush over the world I have built. I love you so much, and I am so thankful to have you by my side as I grow and navigate uncharted territory.

Thank you to my massive list of friends who listen to my stories, show up for events and signings, and support me without hesitation! Baylee, Allison, Emily, Lily, Kayla, Katie, Cassidi, Matthew, Carson, Daniel, Terry, Ashton, Courtney, and Kaitlyn– thank you a million times over for being so absolutely wonderful.

I also want to take a moment to highlight my mom, who makes sure that she always has time to read my books, support me whenever and however she can, and help me puzzle through the intricate web that I have woven this world to be.

Deciding to put my stories down on paper was a surprisingly difficult decision to make, but it is one that I hold no regrets for. I have met so many amazing people during this journey and I will forever be grateful to all of the people who give these books a chance. Knowing that my words have impacted people so deeply has been more than I could ever have dreamed.

I say all of this to highlight the very theme of this book. There is always a choice, dear reader. Sometimes they are easy to make, sometimes they are difficult, and sometimes we regret them.

But always, there is a choice.

ABOUT THE AUTHOR

H.T. Mejia has a passion for animals and has worked in Veterinary Medicine for many years. She is a food enthusiast, a lover of all things fantasy, and she is fascinated with Greek Mythology. H.T. Mejia is the author of The Requiem of Kora duology. She started her author journey at the beginning of 2024.

www.ingramcontent.com/pod-product-compliance
Lightning Source LLC
Chambersburg PA
CBHW050334110726
47899CB00007B/2494